To her horror, she'd been completely misunderstood!

After their night together, Liam promised to give Gina anything. And when she told him of her daughter's desperate need for expensive surgery, his face emptied of all emotion.

"So, the race has been run and you got what you needed," he said tonelessly. "Underneath it all, most people are the same. Don't worry, my dear, the money is no problem. You deserve it. You gave a great performance." His face twisted with self-contempt. "Stupid of me. I've always had a blind spot where you're concerned."

"Liam, no! You mustn't think that. It wasn't a performance!" Gina gasped. "Listen to me—"

But he wouldn't. He thrust a check into her hands, then furiously left the room.

EMMA DARCY nearly became an actress until her fiancé declared he preferred to attend the theater *with* her. She became a wife and mother. Later she took up oil painting—unsuccessfully, she remarks. Then, she tried architecture, designing the family home in New South Wales. Next came romance writing—"the hardest and most challenging of all the activities," she confesses.

Books by Emma Darcy

HARLEQUIN PRESENTS

960—WOMAN OF HONOUR
984—DON'T ASK ME NOW
999—THE UNPREDICTABLE MAN
1020—THE WRONG MIRROR
1033—THE ONE THAT GOT AWAY
1048—STRIKE AT THE HEART
1080—THE POSITIVE APPROACH
1103—MISTRESS OF PILLATORO
1151—ALWAYS LOVE

HARLEQUIN ROMANCE

2900—BLIND DATE
2941—WHIRLPOOL OF PASSION

Don't miss any of our special offers. Write to us at the following address for information on our newest releases.

Harlequin Reader Service
901 Fuhrmann Blvd., P.O. Box 1397, Buffalo, NY 14240
Canadian address: P.O. Box 603,
Fort Erie, Ont. L2A 5X3

EMMA DARCY

a priceless love

Harlequin Books

TORONTO • NEW YORK • LONDON
AMSTERDAM • PARIS • SYDNEY • HAMBURG
STOCKHOLM • ATHENS • TOKYO • MILAN

Harlequin Presents first edition June 1989
ISBN 0-373-11177-0

Original hardcover edition published in 1988
by Mills & Boon Limited

CHAPTER ONE

'GINA...'

A hand gently squeezed her shoulder, forcing her into semi-wakefulness. Another day to face...more work...so much money to earn...so little time. Gina groaned and buried her face in the pillow, wanting to hide behind a few more minutes of precious sleep. She was so tired, so...

'Gina!'

The voice was stridently insistent this time, and the hand shook her unmercifully. Gina's subconscious rebellion faded into the limbo of spent dreams. There was no escaping the driving necessity of what she had to do.

She rolled over and stared blearily at the brilliant orange scattiness of Esme's hair. Gradually her eyes focused on the face that would never launch a thousand ships, but was a marvellous expression of all the positive things in life. It smiled in sympathetic understanding.

'Time to move. I've brought you a cup of coffee.'

'Thanks,' Gina breathed tiredly and forced her legs out from under the bedclothes.

'Late night?' The question held a note of concern.

Gina brushed it off with a shrug. 'Not too bad.'

Esme shook her head. 'You'll have to give this up, Gina. Three jobs...it's just too much. Even for you. And starting off the day without breakfast...you're down to skin and bone!'

An ironic smile twisted Gina's mouth. Esme was built like a matriarchal Amazon. Her six-foot frame carried a formidable amount of flesh, but the biggest part of her was her heart. Ever since she had taken Gina and Debbie under her voluminous wing, Esme had been clucking over how little food they ate.

'I had a big meal last night,' Gina consoled her. 'And I'm not giving it up, Esme. I'll do whatever I have to do to save Debbie's eyesight.'

'Won't help if you lose your health,' Esme grumbled, moving to the wardrobe to get out Gina's work clothes.

Gina sipped the hot coffee, ignoring the comment. However valid it might be, it wasn't pertinent yet. She would hold on to her good health through sheer force of will, if necessary.

'Did you have any trouble?'

'What with?' She hadn't followed Esme's train of thought.

'The Italian gent you had to look after last night.'

Gina shook her head in exasperation. 'Of course not! The company makes it very clear from the start that it won't tolerate any nonsense from its clients. Mr Vincente was small and round, and well into his fifties. And very much the continental gentleman.'

To settle Esme's persistent worries completely, she added, 'It was really a very easy evening. Mr Vincente spoke excellent English. I didn't have to use my Italian at all. The trouble he has in Sydney is understanding the Australian accent. And we talk too fast for him. Anyhow, I made sure he got where he wanted to go and checked everything so he didn't get ripped off anywhere. It was all quite ego-pampering, actually. He had really beautiful manners.'

'Hmmph!' said Esme. 'You've got to be careful of these Latin types. What about the guy that propositioned you?'

'That was his own idea. And he very quickly backed off,' Gina shot back testily, then softened her voice, ashamed of her short temper in the face of Esme's caring nature. 'Please stop worrying about me. The company really does vet these people.'

Esme frowned at her. 'The trouble is, you're too good-looking. All men get ideas when...'

Gina shot her a teasing grin. 'I thought I was skin and bone.'

It won a smile. 'Artistic skin and bone.'

'Art is the word,' Gina said drily. 'It was all Mr Vincente talked about last night. The glories of Rome and Florence and Venice. He was lonely for home and didn't want to know anything about Sydney or Australia. He just wanted a sympathetic ear.' She flashed a look of triumph at her friend and confidante. 'And he was so grateful for it, he gave me a fifty-dollar tip. I don't get that kind of bonus from my other jobs.'

'I can't argue with that,' Esme admitted.

She was in total sympathy with Gina's goal, despite her concern over the toll it was taking on her young friend's life.

No matter how long it took and what she had to do, Gina was determined that her daughter was not going to be blind for the rest of her life. The problem was that the operation Debbie needed to restore her eyesight had to be done in Los Angeles.

The diagnosis of a supracella cyst pressing on the optic chiasma had been alarming enough, but, as the cyst grew, its pressure increased, and Debbie saw less and less. Although the doctors had warned Gina that the surgery offered only a fifty-fifty chance of restoring full vision, it was still worth any sacrifice. Her biggest worry was how far Debbie's condition might deteriorate before she could accumulate the money necessary for the operation.

But what more could she manage? With the help Esme gave them, they lived on a shoestring budget. Gina did office work all week, waitressing at the weekend, and took every evening job the company offered her.

'If only I could speak Japanese,' she sighed. 'The company gets more Japanese businessmen and tourists as clients than any other nationality. I'd get a lot more work from them if I could learn that language, Esme. I wonder if there's a course at...'

'Gina! You can't take on any more,' Esme protested vehemently.

Gina lifted a belligerently determined face, and Esme shook her head. 'I know you're thinking of Debbie's good, but she also needs to see her mother occasionally.'

The point struck home. She was out so much that Debbie was beginning to regard Esme as her mother instead of... Gina swallowed some more coffee and blinked back the tears that had welled into her eyes. Tears of fatigue, she told herself.

'Where's Debbie?' she asked.

'In the kitchen, listening to the cartoons on TV.'

Listening, Gina thought with a twinge of despair. Would she ever see properly again?

'One day I'll sell a painting,' Esme declared, breaking into Gina's morose thoughts with a bright ray of optimism.

'Any day now, Esme,' Gina replied, playing the game with her. It was an old, old game now, but it always helped to lift her spirits. Esme never gave up hope; yet, for all her talent, somehow her paintings never quite worked. In all honesty, Gina could not really like them herself, but she would have died under torture rather than admit it.

'Why is it that artists have to die before their genius is recognised?' came the plaintive cry.

'It's a wicked plot to profit from their talent.' Gina put down the coffee mug and rose to give the big-hearted woman an affectionate hug. 'I think you're a genius, Esme. A noble genius.'

'Better get moving. You'll miss the bus,' was the gruff answer.

Gina raced off to the bathroom, wondering what on earth they would have done without Esme this past year. There could be no one else in the world quite like Esme Follingarth: startlingly eccentric, brutally frank, totally uninhibited, but with a generosity of spirit that swamped any possible criticism of her. She shored up all the frightening spaces in their lives and fed them hope for the future.

A bemused little smile lingered on Gina's mouth as she brushed her long, black hair and applied some colour to her pale face. Meeting Esme had been the best thing that had ever happened to her, although at the time it had been more like meeting a bulldozer.

Debbie had told her about the big, fat lady who came to visit at the Camperdown Children's Hospital. Apparently she enthralled all the children with her stories and accompanying pictures. She had virtually accosted Gina one afternoon—a huge, billowing figure in her bizarrely coloured caftan, dyed-orange hair massed into a lopsided bun which didn't have enough pins to contain it. 'What are you going to do about Debbie?' she had demanded.

And the wondrous part of that blunt, intrusive question was that Esme had cared—really cared—about the answer.

The hard, cold walls of independence that Gina had built to contain her aching loneliness had wobbled and fallen to the power of that caring. It recalled, all too poignantly, her first meeting with Jim so long ago...the heart-curling way he had looked at her and cared about who she was, what she was doing with her life, wanting her to share it with him. She had wanted that caring so much. It was why she had chosen to marry Jim; loving him for loving her, needing the sense of security that came with no longer being alone.

But Jim had died two years ago, unexpectedly, shockingly, and without having made any provision for a future that went on without him. That lack of foresight had not even been a matter for consideration in the first months of her grief for her husband. At least Jim had left her with a daughter to love, and Gina was perfectly capable of supporting them both.

However, it wasn't simply a matter of making a living now, not since Debbie's eye problem had been diagnosed, and no one had really wanted to know about her despair over that ever-mounting problem. No one cared enough.

But Esme did.

And Gina had not been able to stem the flood of response that Esme drew without any of the superficial sympathy that other people had mouthed from time to time. The big woman had simply opened her great heart and invited Gina in—listening, understanding, wanting to know everything, caring.

The pain, the worry, the tortured feeling of helplessness—Gina had poured it all out. She had tried every avenue suggested to her in the hope of raising the fifty thousand dollars needed to take Debbie to the United States for the necessary operation. There was no charity that covered this specific problem. It wasn't a matter of life and death, just a little girl's failing eyesight; not cause enough to open the public's purse. The burden sat squarely and heavily on Gina's shoulders.

And she had shouldered it as best she could: fighting back despair whenever the task ahead of her seemed impossible and clinging on to her determination to get the money somehow...some way. She had given up the pleasant apartment that she and Jim had rented, and had taken the cheapest lodgings she'd been able to find, but still the cost of living had been high with having to pay for Debbie's care while she'd worked during the day. What savings she'd made seemed pitiable against the amount she needed.

Gina had racked her brains to come up with alternative ways of making money, but she had found no satisfactory answer to bettering their situation.

'You have no family to turn to?' Esme had frowned in questioning concern.

Tears had swum into Gina's eyes. Jim had been an orphan, she explained. As for herself, she had been the only child of divorced parents, cared for by her Italian grandmother while her mother worked to keep them. Gina had lost them both in the Granville railway disaster which had tragically claimed so many other lives. Her father did not come forward at the time, nor did she know where he was. Gina had managed on her own until Jim had come along and married her... Jim with his promise of forever love.

He *had* loved her. Gina had never doubted that, despite her private frustrations over some aspects of their relationship. And they had been so happy when Debbie was born; their very own child, a beautiful baby daughter. Jim had adored her. If only they had known what was going to happen...

But it was too late now to wish things had been done differently. Jim was dead, and he had died before Debbie's eye problem had even been suspected, let alone diagnosed. He had neglected to invest in any insurance, and throughout their marriage he had spent all their spare cash on chasing a dream... a dream that had cost him his life in the end.

There was no one she could turn to, Gina had whispered despairingly to Esme, tears trickling down her cheeks.

'You come and live with me,' had been Esme's prompt solution, and it had been more in the nature of an order than a suggestion. 'I can't give you money. Haven't got any. I barely scrape a living out of my paintings. But I have got a terraced house in Paddington that my father left me, and a spare room for you and Debbie. No rent, and I'll look after Debbie free of charge.'

Gina's embarrassed protests had been met by Esme's rollicking laugh. 'I love kids. Couldn't have any myself. And Debbie's a little darling. Can't have her going blind when there's all the world to see.'

And she had scornfully dismissed the suggestion that caring for Debbie might be too much for her. 'You're only as old as you feel,' had been Esme's retort, refusing to recognise any limitations. The grey roots of her orange hair placed her at somewhere between forty and sixty, but she had such an ageless quality in her joy of living that Debbie had never regarded her as a grandmother figure, but as a playmate. Her greeting every morning was, 'What are we going to do today, Esme?' And she was never disappointed with Esme's answer.

They were lucky, incredibly lucky that Esme had taken them in, and taken them over in lots of ways. If only there wasn't the ever-pressing problem of earning enough money... Gina stifled another sigh, dashed on some lipstick and hurried back to the bedroom.

Five minutes later she was dressed in the white blouse and black skirt which were standard uniform for her job in the stockbroker's office. A glance at her watch showed that she barely had time to say goodbye to Debbie before dashing to the bus-stop. She clattered downstairs to the combined kitchen and living-room, and swept her four-year-old daughter up into her arms.

'I've got to go, darling,' she said breathlessly.

'You smell nice, Mummy,' Debbie smiled in delight.

Gina felt a tight constriction in her throat as she caressed the mop of black curls and looked into the nearly sightless green eyes. Debbie was the image of herself as a child, except for... 'Be a good girl for Esme,' she whispered.

'We're going shopping,' Debbie informed her happily.

'I wish I could go, too,' Gina said huskily. 'Bye, now.'

'Bye, Mummy.' She planted a wet kiss on Gina's cheek and slithered down from her mother's embrace.

Gina's heart ached as she watched her daughter settle complacently in front of the television again. Debbie didn't seem to miss her at all. Not that Gina wanted her to, but...

'Better eat this apple on the bus,' Esme advised.

'I'm not hungry,' Gina said distractedly.

'Eat it!' Esme commanded, thrusting it into Gina's hand. 'You might not feel like it, but you need it. You can't keep burning the candle at both ends and in the middle unless...'

'All right, all right,' Gina agreed, already on her way to the door at the tactful reminder that the bus would not wait for her.

She was just in time to catch it, and lucky enough to get a seat. Paddington was only ten minutes away from the business-heart of the city, but the morning traffic was always heavy, and Gina had stolidly munched through the apple and re-applied her lipstick before she had to alight.

Jepherson, Jepherson and Potts, Stockbrokers of Sydney, were situated in a prestigious building close to the Stock Exchange. Gina liked working there as a secretary-receptionist. It was quiet, not like her waitressing job at the weekends. And she could sit down all day, which was even better. On the whole she was managing everything very well, she told herself as she took the elevator up to the fourth floor.

Two hours later, Gina was lulled into a peaceful frame of mind by a pile of mechanical paperwork which was gradually diminishing. All she had to concentrate on was getting the right contracts into the right envelopes. There had been nothing to disturb the pleasant tenor of the morning's work, and it looked like being a very easy day. No problem at all.

'Well, well! Look who we have here!'

The insolently arrogant drawl raised the hairs on the back of Gina's neck. She knew that voice. She hadn't heard it for years, but recognition was instant. It could only belong to one person. Even before she looked up, she could see him in her mind's eye.

Liam Shannon.

Her husband's *best* friend. The hero of the orphanage where he and Jim had grown up. The man who could do no wrong, as far as Jim had been able to see. But Gina had known better. No *best* friend would ever have acted as Liam Shannon had done!

She could not imagine what had brought him into this building, to this office where she worked. Probably an ill wind, Gina thought in bitter resentment. She fiercely wished it would blow him back out again and sweep him off to wherever he had been all these years. And keep him there!

He had walked out of their lives on the day she had married Jim—after he had caused that dreadful scene—and while Jim had often speculated about what Liam might be doing, Gina had worked hard at shutting her mind to any thought of him. And she didn't want him disturbing her now, either. Liam Shannon was no good.

She took a deep breath and tried to control the hostility that was surging through her. Slowly she raised her eyes from her desk and levelled her gaze at the man lounging in the doorway.

Six years hadn't changed him. He was still as handsome as the devil himself: the thick black hair, riotously curly and flopping on to his forehead, inviting every woman to flick it up; the wickedly challenging arch of his eyebrows above teasing blue eyes; a strong, straight nose with just that slight flare of nostrils that suggested passion; a full-lipped, sensual mouth that promised everything; and an aggressively masculine jawline that was broken by the tantalising cleft in his chin.

His dark grey three-piece business-suit was a sober mockery of the essential non-conformity of the man. The scarlet silk tie was a truer reflection of his personality...a bright, vibrant red for danger! Where Liam Shannon was concerned, nothing was safe or sacred. Why he aroused such violent emotions in her, Gina did not know. Nor had she ever tried to analyse it. He just did. And some deep-

rooted instinct shrieked that she never reveal what
he wrought inside her.

Drawing from years of self-discipline, Gina
exerted almost superhuman control on herself. No
line of expression showed on the smooth, pale skin
of her oval face. With studied disdain, she slowly
raised one delicately arched eyebrow.

'Can I help you, Liam?' she asked, her tone
devoid of anything but professional politeness, as
though she had last seen him yesterday.

He sauntered into the reception office with the
same old king-of-the-walk manner that Gina found
so offensive. The sheer cockiness of the man made
her hackles rise. Liam Shannon never took second
place to anyone. He didn't give a damn for man,
or bird, or beast. And he certainly didn't give a
damn about her!

'You remember me,' he said, propping himself
on her desk and flashing her the smile that was
geared to have the same devastating effect as a
neutron bomb.

She had to remain cool. He was trying to stir her,
to get reactions that fed his monumental ego. He
would take advantage of any crack in her
composure.

She counted to ten, and then to twenty. Stay
cool, she recited after every number. Fifteen...
sixteen... seventeen... She needed this job, and if
she erupted, as she was bursting to, it would cause
a frightful scene. She had enough experience of
Liam Shannon to know that he would never back

off. Given half a chance, he would devour her like a piranha.

Somehow Gina managed to clamp down on her emotions. She even pasted a plastic smile on her face. 'Impossible not to remember you, Liam,' she flicked at him, trying to give the words a hint of contempt.

His eyes flashed wickedly, as if her answer pleased him.

Hers froze over. 'I'll never forget what you did on my wedding day. I doubt I will ever forgive you.'

He gave no sign that the words meant anything to him at all. But of course he wouldn't care, Gina reminded herself, struggling to contain her rising temper. Liam Shannon only recognised his own needs and feelings. Hers had never counted with him. Nor had Jim's, despite the claim of friendship.

For her own peace of mind she had to get rid of him, and as quickly as possible. If Mr Jepherson came out and saw her wasting her time with Liam Shannon, he would leap to a lot of ill-founded conclusions. 'I'm very busy...' she began, wanting to drop her gaze, to ignore him, yet unable to break the battle of wills that kept her eyes locked to his.

The smile left his face. He reached across and picked up her hands from the desk, folding them powerfully within his own. The impulse to jerk away from him was too strong and immediate for Gina to restrain. She pulled with all her might, half rising from her seat with the effort. His fingers tightened with inexorable purpose. He held her easily.

'It's been a long time, Gina. Too long!'

She felt again the waves of restrained violence she had sensed in Liam Shannon every time she had met him.

'Please let me go.' To be forcibly held in her office like this...if a client came in and saw them, it would look so bad! Gina struggled frantically to free herself.

His hands held her even more firmly. Gina found his icy calm unnerving, like the unnatural stillness before nature unleashed its most destructive elements. She stopped struggling, her innate pride forcing her to accept defeat with dignity.

The slight smile on Liam's face was completely lacking in warmth. 'And how is Jim?' he asked, his tone of polite enquiry mocking the force he was still plying with ruthless efficiency.

'My husband died two years ago.' Gina paused to shaft the shot home. 'Doing what you taught him.'

The smile on his face faded into nothingness, a ghost of the past...wiped out. His utter stillness held the eerie quality of time being suspended. A shiver ran down Gina's spine. It was as if some elemental force was changing course...worlds in collision...remoulding...forming another universe.

His eyes glittered with some indecipherable emotion. 'Tell me about it.' The austere command brooked no evasion.

She didn't want to talk about Jim. Not to Liam Shannon. But she also had to get rid of him from the office. Recognising that she had no other choice but to give in, Gina made the summary as brief as possible.

'Jim tried for a long-distance gliding record. There was a fault in the design. The wing roots were over-stressed . . . he crashed into a hill.'

Bitterness surged over the pain of those stark words. All her problems had started after Jim's death. And she owed Liam Shannon nothing. She hoped that just this once she had struck through his hard, self-sufficient shell, and pierced his feckless heart.

'Now, please go,' she hissed at him through clenched teeth.

He didn't move. Her eyes fiercely challenged him, but he didn't speak either. He studied her for long, silent, nerve-tearing moments. His gaze lifted to the centre-parting of her lustrous black hair, and drifted down the rippling waves to her shoulders. It dropped to the thrust of her breasts under the white silk blouse and the still-trim waist emphasised by the band of her black skirt.

Gina wanted to scream at him to stop it, but a vice seemed to have clamped around her throat. She couldn't even breathe. Her ears vaguely acknowledged the muffled roar of the city traffic outside, but the thundering beat of her heart was much louder.

His gaze travelled slowly up the line of her shirt-buttons to the long column of her throat, then lingered on the sweet curves of her small mouth until her lips pressed together in vexation. He surveyed the disdainful tilt of her dainty *retroussée* nose and finally met the blazing resentment in her darkly fringed green eyes.

He released her hands, and Gina sank gratefully back into her chair.

'At least he had the pleasure of having you,' he said bitterly, and the glittering taunt in his eyes held the savage desire to crack her defences.

To her utter mortification, a hot flush crept up her neck and burnt into her cheeks. 'Have you no feelings at all?' she cried in ravaged protest, and when his mouth curled slightly to one side, she could not contain herself any longer. 'I don't think I could dislike anyone more intensely than I do you, Liam.'

A tightness hardened his face. His hands clenched into fists. His eyes darkened to a stormy indigo, threatening an explosive bolt of lightning at any moment.

'I have feelings,' he said in a voice that gave throbbing emphasis to every word, 'and they're just as intense as yours. Don't you find that curious, Gina?'

The last vestige of her control snapped. 'Get out, Liam! Just go and leave me alone. You've got no business here, and I never want to see you again.'

'That's too bad!' he mocked. 'Because I want to see you, Gina, and with Jim gone, there's nothing now to stop me.'

He smiled like a shark that scented blood, then strolled over to the door to read the inscription out loud. 'Stockbrokers. Jepherson, Jepherson and

Potts. Well, a few stocks and shares won't go astray. I'll come here to buy some every day. Just to see you, Gina.'

Her stomach twisted into knots. She could not let him do that to her! In sheer defensive desperation, she forced a laugh from her dry throat. This was her best strategy... to defuse the whole encounter by injecting a light, inconsequential tone that proved her indifference to his threat.

'This is out of your class, Liam. You can't afford what we're selling.'

Liam Shannon had never had money. He spent it on one madcap scheme after another. It was a wonder he could even afford the suit he was wearing.

He swung back to her, emanating male aggression. 'I can afford anything I want.'

Let him be hoist with his own petard, Gina thought, wanting him to pay for his presumption. 'Then I'll make an appointment for you. Right now,' she said acidly, determined to get rid of him one way or another.

His eyes bored into hers, promising a challenge to the last drop of blood between them. 'Make it the senior Mr Jepherson. Perhaps I'll even buy this business. I rather fancy being your boss, Gina.'

Talking big, just as he had always done. Even when he was flat broke. 'I'll just check if he's free,' Gina said smoothly, hiding the malice that was welling into her heart as she picked up the telephone and punched the line-buttons.

The senior Mr. Jepherson was all of sixty years old, and probably the most conservative stock-broker in Australia. Liam would get little joy out of him! They would mix like fire and water, and the inevitable quenching might teach Liam Shannon a much-needed lesson.

New clients were relatively uncommon in these straitened times and, as Gina expected, satisfaction oozed from Mr Jepherson's voice. 'Hold him there. I'll be right out.'

She smiled up at Liam. 'He'll see you immediately.'

Liam removed a card from his wallet. 'That's my business address.' His eyes taunted her with wicked suggestiveness. 'For pleasure, I stay elsewhere while I'm in Sydney.'

'I bet you do!' Gina slid out, all too well aware of how Liam Shannon derived his pleasure. Her own experience with him had been enough to confirm all the tales that Jim had told her.

Mr Jepherson made a timely entrance; he was a short, thick-set man with large jowls and white hair. His face beamed with pleasure as Gina effected the introductions. Liam looked back at her with a satisfied expression as he was drawn towards the inner sanctum of the elderly stockbroker.

'Have you any recommendations in the equity field, Gina? Something above all else that I should buy?'

The urge to pay him back for all the pain he had caused her was overwhelming. Without stopping to consider what she was doing, Gina promptly answered, 'Try NECSEC, Mr Shannon.'

Revenge was sweet. Of course, he wouldn't do it. But, if he did, he would be really flying high on that one. And dropping to rock-bottom. It was the most horrendous share on the market.

She smiled. 'I'm sure they're about to discover something really brilliant.'

Mr Jepherson shot her a beetling frown, and almost pushed Liam into his office. 'I can't possibly advise NECSEC, Mr Shannon. My secretary doesn't know what she's talking about,' he rumbled as he shut the door behind them.

A stupid impulse, Gina chided herself. She had won no points with her employer, who would very quickly dissuade his new client from investing his money in anything so unwise as that particular exploration company.

She propped her elbows on her desk and wearily dropped her face into her hands. She had made an utter mess of this meeting with Liam. Maybe even a mess of her job. And how on earth was she going to handle him if Liam Shannon carried out his threats and came to visit her every day?

CHAPTER TWO

GINA rubbed at her temples, trying to compose herself. Whatever malicious trick of fate had brought Liam Shannon to this office, she had certainly compounded the problem by losing control of the situation. To waste so much energy on a man like him was the height of stupidity. It gained her nothing and turned her into a nervous wreck.

She reminded herself that Liam Shannon was without honour or decency. He had stirred explosive emotions in her right from the first moment she had set eyes on him . . . or from the moment he had set eyes on her! Even though Jim had warned her that his best friend was a devil with women, she hadn't expected to be treated so . . . so disrespectfully. Not when she was Jim's fiancée, and Liam was supposed to be Jim's best friend!

He had made her seethe with indignation, undressing her with his eyes, not even trying to disguise his lecherous interest in her body. And when he had cut in on Jim, demanding a dance with her, the way he had moved his body against hers . . . so disgustingly intimate.

Jim had been deaf, dumb and blind not to see Liam Shannon for what he was. Liam had actually gone so far as to proposition her a week before the wedding! And then to turn up drunk at the church when he was Jim's *best man* . . . Gina had been terrified throughout the whole wedding reception that he would say or do something shamefully outrageous.

And he had! A kiss for the bride! He had moved his mouth sensually over hers, forcing her lips open and . . . even the memory of it made her chest heave with revulsion and her pulse quicken with anger. It had been like a rape of all her senses, a violent assault on all that she was. She had slapped him, right in front of all the guests.

Jim had tried to draw him away, smooth the incident over, but Liam had knocked his arm aside and left, without an apology to anyone. Gina hadn't seen him from that day to this. And neither had Jim.

She had been intensely relieved that he had never come near them again, although Jim had been hurt by the dropping of their friendship. Loyal to a fault—and there had been other more grievous faults in her husband that she had not known about on the day they were married—but Jim had nursed a blind faith in Liam Shannon.

'One day he'll be big, Gina. He said he'd do it, and by God, he will! There's a man for you!' he had declared admiringly.

Not for me, thank you, Gina had silently sworn, and eventually Jim had become disillusioned when he finally realised that Liam Shannon had ruthlessly cut him out of his life.

Jim had never wanted to face up to the unpleasant, or even the practical things of life. He had loved with a childish trust that everything should work out right, and if occasionally she had felt let-down or dissatisfied with the realities of their relationship, Jim had only to turn his look of loving appeal on her and she had readily forgiven him his shortcomings. He had been a good person: impulsively generous and kind, always happy to lend a hand with anything, never meaning anyone harm.

The same could not be said of Liam Shannon!

Gina's jaw tightened. She was not going to let him disrupt her life. And right now, her job was the important thing. Mr Jepherson was displeased with her as it was—she hoped not too badly. If she didn't get today's contracts word-processed in time, she wouldn't be holding this job for much longer.

Gina applied herself to the work in hand, determined not to be found wanting when Mr Jepherson re-appeared. She was tired. That was the trouble. Tired and on edge, and all too prone to do stupid things.

Suggesting NECSEC to Liam in front of Mr Jepherson had been a reckless indiscretion, a self-indulgence brought on by fatigue. Maybe Esme was right and she couldn't handle three jobs. But she had to cope with them. Had to!

Gina's head bent studiously over her task as she heard Mr Jepherson's door open. She wasn't going to make any more trouble for herself by opening her mouth in front of her boss.

'I would like to see your secretary for a few minutes, Mr Jepherson,' Liam demanded pleasantly, knowing all too well that he wouldn't be refused.

'So would I.' Mr Jepherson's response held a decidedly baleful note.

Gina glanced up warily.

Liam grinned at her. 'I took your advice, Mrs York, and bought into NECSEC.'

Her heart plummeted. She wasn't game to look beyond him. 'I...er...hope you don't regret it, Mr Shannon.'

'Oh, I'm sure I won't. I got twenty-five thousand,' he said, so blithely that she suspected the worst kind of skulduggery behind the purchase.

Gina did a quick calculation. At two cents a share, that worked out at five hundred dollars. Liam's suit would have cost him that much, and the business was so small by Mr Jepherson's standards that he could surely overlook this one little indiscretion on her part.

She smiled in sheer relief. 'Well, you could have a surprising result, Mr Shannon. Twenty-five thousand shares is a nice little investment.'

'Dollars, Mrs York,' Mr Jepherson said to Gina, emphasising every word. 'Not shares. Dollars!' He looked to be on the verge of apoplexy. 'Please see me in my office when Mr Shannon leaves.' The slam of his door punctuated the depth of his displeasure.

Gina felt sick. That was her job gone. There was nothing more certain. And Liam Shannon had deliberately done it to her. God knew where he had got the money from! Most probably he didn't have it at all, which made it even worse! Mr Jepherson would have spent his valuable time trying to talk him out of it, and more than likely the whole transaction was nothing but a con-job!

She had given Liam enough rope and—damn his eyes!—he had hung her with it. Damn him! Damn his wicked mind and all that he was, right down to his black soul!

And he had the extra brass to hitch himself on to her desk again and grin at her, obviously delighted with his mischief.

'How about coming out with me tonight to celebrate our little investment?'

The beastly gall of the man left Gina speechless with rage.

'What time shall I pick you up?' he burbled on, taking her acceptance for granted.

She wanted to scratch his teasing eyes out, but somehow she dredged up some shreds of control. 'I'm not free, Liam.'

'Why not?'

Because Debbie needed all her time, because she had to work, because... because... because she didn't like the man! She had to get him out of her life once and for all. Gina made a supreme intellectual effort to come up with an answer that would leave her free of him for ever. Something he couldn't argue with, something guaranteed to crush him and his enormous ego.

'I'm having dinner with my... lover.' The word was hard to say, and it was even more difficult trying to force a provocative little smile of satisfaction on to her face . . . as if it was something she was looking forward to.

Liam didn't even blink. 'Afterwards, then?' There was a silky edge to his voice, as if he knew she was lying.

It made Gina feel defeated, but she rallied once more to the challenge. She was committed now. She stared at him without so much as a flicker of evasion. 'After that, I'm going to bed with him. All night. There's no room in my life for you, Liam. No . . .'

'Tomorrow night?'

'Not tomorrow night, nor the next, nor any night. I am totally committed. Is that clear, Liam? I'll never have free time for you! Never!'

It wiped the sparkle from his eyes, but Gina's brief triumph was seared away by the blaze of purpose that replaced it. A muscle twitched beneath his cheekbone.

'One of these days, your head is going to stop ruling your heart, Gina,' he mocked in a soft, tight, infinitely dangerous voice. 'And that beautiful body of yours will be mine.'

He raised his hand as if to touch her face, and Gina flinched away.

He laughed. 'Ask yourself why you fear it so much, Gina.'

'I hate you, Liam Shannon.' Her voice literally shook with the force of her emotion.

He raised a sardonic eyebrow and languidly removed himself from her desk. 'I feel pretty strongly about you too,' he drawled, tipping her a mocking salute before turning away.

She watched him walk to the door and knew that he had got the better of her once again. Why did he stir such volatile reactions from her? It wasn't right. It wasn't good. The regular circuitry of her body went haywire in Liam Shannon's presence, as if he projected a magnetic force that continually attacked order and common sense. She hoped he would never cross her path again.

He turned and caught her gaze on him, and a triumphant grin spread across his face. 'I'll be back tomorrow. If not before. I haven't felt so exhilarated for a long time.'

His eyes danced with satanic pleasure, and for several seconds after he left Gina sat riveted to her chair, wishing she had thought of some final retort that would have flattened him.

With a heavy sigh, she pushed herself to her feet. Mr Jepherson's wrath had to be faced, and he was probably getting more wrathful with every minute that passed. And what explanation could she give for her idiocy? Who could explain Liam Shannon?

It was strange, but Liam had left her feeling so listless and drained she couldn't bring herself to care about her job. Not now. She would later, she knew. When it was too late.

Mr Jepherson gave her no chance to explain anything. With an icy dignity that shut the door on all possible excuses, he told her he would not have his secretary usurping his function to recommend stock to clients. He would prefer it if she sought a job elsewhere. He would give her that opportunity immediately. She could leave right now. And to facilitate her departure he wrote her a cheque that more than covered her holiday and severance pay.

Gina made no attempt to argue. Mr Jepherson would never understand the kind of game Liam played. Besides, by removing her from this office, he also removed her from the field of combat. Liam Shannon would not find her here when he came back tomorrow.

A dull weariness settled over her as Gina cleared her desk of all personal items. She decided not to bother looking for another job today. She felt too depressed to present herself to her best advantage at any interviews. Tomorrow she would be on top of things again.

The cheque in her handbag was a comfort to her as she took the elevator down to the street-level foyer. If she could get another job quickly, Gina calculated that, as far as money in the bank was concerned, she would have gained more than she had lost. Unfortunately, Mr Jepherson hadn't given her a reference and she hadn't dared ask for one. However, she would find a way around that.

Gina was considering various ideas as she stepped out on to the marble floor of the foyer, but all thought fled instantly from her mind when she lifted her gaze and saw him again. His eyes were boring straight into her. Gina's heart stopped dead. And so did her feet.

With the lethal air of a machine gun swinging into action, Liam Shannon rose from the armchair which had been so handily situated between the bank of elevators and the exit doors. He blocked her escape path with a few steps, and covered the space between them before Gina had regathered wits enough to make a move.

'That didn't take long,' he said, hooking his arm around hers and smiling his satisfaction. 'I do like people to perform as I direct them. It was cheaper to buy the shares than Jepherson's business. And now that I've ensured that you have plenty of free time, Gina, I'll take you out to lunch.'

The smug admission that he had deliberately manipulated Mr Jepherson into sacking her sent a violent shot of adrenalin through Gina's veins. 'You rotter...' she snapped, and tried to yank her arm out of his.

When that failed, she swung her other arm at his face. He caught her wrist and forcibly lowered it. 'You started this war, Gina. Now you're going to watch me win it!'

'I don't want a war with you!' she seethed. 'God damn you, Liam! Let me go, or I'll create a scene you'll rue to the day you...'

He pulled her hard against him and smothered her mouth with his. Gina's arms were helplessly pinned within his embrace, and there was nothing she could do to stop him. One of his hands had thrust under her hair to clamp the back of her head still; the other was spread over the small of her back, relentlessly pressing her into an intimate awareness of his muscular physique.

To her utter shame, the sheer aggressive maleness of his body awakened a flood of sexual needs that Gina had almost forgotten. And his mouth, after its first bruising impact, was working on hers with pulse-jolting sensuality. She kept her teeth clenched, remembering all too vividly the shattering invasion of his kiss on her wedding day, but that didn't stop Liam from ravaging the sensitive inner tissues of her lips and stirring feelings that opened up a frightening well of vulnerability.

Little quivers of weakness ran down her thighs. Her empty stomach was hit by a series of quick contractions. Her heart clamoured wildly for release. Her breasts ached with sensitivity. She wanted to open her mouth. Only the most deep-rooted pride prevented her from giving that surrender.

'Do what you like, Gina, but I'm going to have you,' Liam breathed as he lifted his head. 'Now make your scene!' he taunted, and the glittering light of challenge in his eyes warned her that she would rue it, not he.

Her chest heaved for breath. She felt so shaken, she could barely think, but retaliation spat from her tongue. 'You are the most despicable, hateful man...'

'So you told me.' His mouth twisted in savage irony. 'When I saw you in your office, I meant to play it cool. But you goad me beyond the bounds of reason and patience. You went too far, Gina. I won't let you deny me again, so don't waste your breath on telling me the lies you tell yourself. The only peace you'll get from me now will be in my bed. After I've had what I want from you.'

'You're mad!' she whispered, frightened by the intensity of his emotions.

'You drive me mad! You always have!' he retorted fiercely. 'But whatever words you say, Gina, your body doesn't hate me. It responds to mine with the same quivering desire it expressed six years ago, from the very first moment we met!'

'No!'

'Want another demonstration?' he threatened. 'Or shall I ask our spectators how it looked to them?'

A wave of heat burnt into Gina's cheeks as she glanced around the foyer to find everyone watching them with absorbed interest. While she was still thrown off guard, Liam took a firm grasp of her elbow and steered her towards the door. He had drawn her several steps before Gina snapped the chains of embarrassment and wrenched herself out of his hold. She whirled on him, spitting defiance.

'I'm not going anywhere with you!'

Liam heaved an exasperated sigh. 'Gina, we have a luncheon engagement that cannot be postponed.' His voice was pitched to a carrying level, inviting everyone to listen to the argument.

'No way!' she breathed in furious resentment. 'There's no way...'

He swooped, scooping her legs out from under her and hoisting her up in his arms.

'Put me down!' she shrieked, bucking and kicking and beating at him with her free arm.

'Lovers' tiff,' Liam blandly told the onlookers, striding on regardless of her blows. 'Mind opening the door for us?' he asked someone over her shoulder.

'No! He's abducting me!' Gina yelled, frantic to establish the truth.

'Perhaps I should take her to bed instead of lunch,' Liam observed to the man who obligingly opened the door.

'No! He means to rape me!' Gina cried in desperate appeal.

'Well, you raped me last time, Gina. It *is* my turn,' Liam declared for everyone to hear.

The man holding the door chuckled.

'Help me, you idiot!' Gina screamed at him.

'Now, now, darling. You'll like it. You truly will,' Liam soothed, carrying her down the steps and across the pavement.

'I hate you, hate you, hate you!' Gina shrieked, thumping him with all her might.

'How can you say that when I love you so much?' Liam said in loud reproach.

Tears of furious frustration sprang into Gina's eyes. No one was coming to her aid, and she couldn't break Liam's inflexible strength. She caught a blurred glimpse of a uniformed chauffeur standing at attention, and then Liam was lowering her into the back seat of a limousine and pushing in after her.

The door was firmly shut. Tinted windows closed out the rest of the world. In sheer panic, Gina scrambled over to the far side of the seat and tried to open the other door. It was locked. A glass partition separated her from the driver's seat. The chauffeur didn't even look at her as he climbed in behind the wheel, and ignored her banging on the glass as he started the motor.

'Relax, my darling,' Liam advised in a voice dripping with silky indulgence. 'I have no intention of raping you. Not yet, anyway. For the present, I'm simply taking you out to lunch.'

CHAPTER THREE

LIAM was undoubtedly in command. He had won this round but, by God, the next would be hers! Angry with herself for having given way to panic for even a few seconds, Gina sank back into the plush leather seat, folded her arms in mutinous patience, crossed her legs to show that she was totally relaxed, and pointedly ignored Liam by staring out the side window.

Disdainful silence—that was her best strategy. It had been a stupid mistake to have ever opened her mouth this morning. War, Liam had called it, and war she would give him, but with a weapon that he couldn't turn against her...passive resistance. There was not much satisfaction to be wrung out of a stone.

The limousine swept up William Street, through King's Cross and down to Rushcutter's Bay. Gina frowned heavily to herself as it pulled up at the marina. She couldn't see any restaurant. The chauffeur opened Liam's door, not hers. Gina did not move.

'If I have to carry you out to my boat, I will,' Liam said with quiet menace. 'Please yourself, Gina.'

He alighted from the car and stood waiting for her to follow. Gina made a quick survey of the marina. The boats were jammed up together. There were people around. She felt confident of being able to get away from Liam if he pushed her too far. She got out of the car, still maintaining a stony silence and an icy dignity.

Again he took a firm grip on her elbow. Gina suffered it without comment. She accompanied him along the jetty with an air of supreme indifference, refusing to look at him or ask which boat was his. He steered her straight to the end of the jetty and started drawing in the mooring rope of a small outboard motor.

'Where are we going?' The words tripped off her tongue before she could catch them back.

He gave her a humourless smile. 'My yacht is anchored in the bay. It provides the privacy I want with you.'

There was only one yacht riding at anchor: a huge, streamlined cruiser that not only looked to be the latest marvel of modern design and technology, but also the acme of millionaire-standard luxury. 'That's yours?' she said incredulously.

'That's mine. And yours to share, if you want to.'

'You've got hopes,' she muttered under her breath. 'And if I refuse to go?' she said out aloud.

'The pleasure will be mine.'

Gina wasn't quite sure what he meant by that, and she preferred not to pursue the matter. Pride insisted that she not be rattled by anything he said or did. She swung herself over the side of the jetty and into the boat. It rocked alarmingly, and she quickly sat down. Liam was right behind her. He unhitched the mooring rope and, without another word to her, went forward and started the engine.

He manoeuvred the boat away from the jetty and opened up the throttles. They sped towards the yacht, and for a few pleasurable moments Gina shut Liam out of her mind and enjoyed the lift of the breeze through her hair, the buoyant ride of the boat through the creaming waves, the sparkle of the midday sun on the expanse of blue harbour beyond the bay.

It was a beautiful day. Fluffy white clouds softened the brilliant azure sky; there was not a sign of city smog anywhere, and it was warm enough to still be summer, although it was late April.

It had been so long since Gina had really noticed how beautiful a day could be, and she breathed in the fresh, salty air with a poignant longing for days past, when the only mission in her life had been living.

If her companion could only have been a friend and not an antagonist . . . but reality was a far cry from the fantasy of happily sharing anything with a man like Liam Shannon.

As the yacht loomed closer, Gina could not help thinking how totally unfair it was that this man could spend millions on a playboy extravagance while Debbie went blind for the sake of fifty thousand dollars. Perhaps if she had been nice to him . . .

Self-derision welled over the thought. She had been incapable of remaining polite for longer than a few seconds. And obviously she stirred as deep an animosity in Liam as he stirred in her. Niceness had always been an impossibility. Any word they had ever spoken to each other held at least a subtle barb designed to get under the skin. Yet he had to feel some kind of compulsive desire for her. His actions today made no other sense.

There were crewmen on the yacht. One of them helped Gina on board, while another tied up the outboard motor.

'I want a cold luncheon sent up for us in the dining-room,' Liam instructed. 'We'll serve ourselves. See that we're not disturbed.'

'Yessir, Mr Shannon, sir!'

Gina rolled her eyes. She bet Liam lapped up that kind of obsequious subservience. She wondered how he had got so filthy rich, but decided not to ask him, because that would only give him the pleasure of telling her and rubbing it in. However, it was difficult not to be impressed when he led her below deck to a fabulously furnished entertainment-room.

The lushly piled carpet was a soft, practical mushroom colour, but there was nothing practical about the pastel leather couches and armchairs: off-white, peach and grey-green, piled with toning and contrasting cushions to offer sumptuous comfort. The occasional tables were pale, polished stone, starkly modern in design, but rich in texture. At the end of the room was a much-mirrored bar, elegantly finished with gleaming brass.

Gina could not help comparing the luxury around her to her own threadbare existence where every cent had to be counted. What bitter irony that the one person of her acquaintance who obviously had the wealth to help Debbie was the one person she could never ask!

Jim would have, without hesitation, but Jim was dead, and Liam had made it all too clear that he intended to capitalise on that fact. If she gave him the slightest opening to wield power over her, he would use it unmercifully. She was sure of that, and she had no reason to suppose he would give her the money anyway. War, he had said, and Gina was not about to give Liam Shannon any advantage whatsoever.

'You do yourself proud, Liam,' she observed with a niggling edge of mockery.

He made no reply and, when she turned around to face him, he was watching her with a narrowed, speculative gaze. His jacket had already been discarded and tossed on to a nearby armchair, and his fingers were busy unbuttoning his waistcoat. Gina's heart skipped a beat.

She did not believe for one moment that Liam meant to force her into his bed. What he really wanted was for her to submit to him. And no way was that going to happen! Nevertheless, she found her gaze drawn to the muscular breadth of his shoulders and quickly looked away.

She waved a careless hand to encompass her surroundings. 'Is this why you've brought me here? To show me what a big man you've become?'

Gina wished she could follow her resolve and keep her mouth shut, but somehow talking helped to stave off her growing awareness that she was really alone with Liam Shannon. For the first time... ever!

'Trying to goad me, Gina?' The words held a soft hint of menace.

She swung hard, angry eyes back to him. 'I'm not trying to do anything to you!' Then, with pent-up frustration over his treatment of her, Gina burst into direct attack. 'Why am I here, Liam? What do you really want?'

With provocative deliberation, he removed his tie and flicked open the top buttons of his shirt. 'I would have thought that was obvious.'

The need to cut Liam Shannon's feet out from under him, to make him see himself as she saw him, welled up in Gina and spilled into a scathing tirade. 'Is it still such a monstrous scar on your ego that you wanted me six years ago and didn't get me? Am I the only woman who's ever rejected you, Liam? Is that the score?' His eyes blazed with sudden fury, but Gina had abandoned all restraint. Scorn poured off her tongue. 'You can't let it go, can you? You've got to be the all-conquering hero! The master! The...'

He gave a harsh bark of laughter that startled her into silence.

'Don't be a fool!' he tossed at her derisively. Then his voice hardened into bitter steel. 'Are you so blind that you can't get anything straight?'

His mouth twisted as he started walking towards her, and the glitter in his eyes was so bright and feverish that Gina warily decided that discretion might very well be the better part of valour. She bit down on her tongue.

'Perhaps you are the only woman who's rejected me, but I wouldn't even know if that's so,' he said with savage irony. 'I've never been sufficiently interested in any other woman to care whether she said yes or no. I don't carve notches in my belt, Gina.'

Stung into defence by his words and approach, Gina cast discretion to the winds. 'I suppose you've had so many falling all over you that...'

'Shut up!' His hands whipped up and cupped her face, enforcing her silence. 'Just shut up and listen for once!'

And the violence she had always sensed in him simmered in his eyes. His voice throbbed with it as his fingers pushed up and down the line of her cheeks in restless wanting. 'I loved you, Gina. Totally. Do you know what that means?'

Loved her! His use of the word instantly stirred a ready scepticism, yet the way he spoke... the turbulent passion in his voice... in his eyes...

'Let me tell you. I loved you with all my being. With all my thoughts and actions. Beyond reason or control. I was crazy for you. Never before or since have I been so possessed by a woman.'

She swallowed, her mind jammed between belief and disbelief. Never had she once imagined that Liam Shannon might actually love her. He had always put her on edge with the lust he had continually projected in a thousand subtle and unsubtle ways. It couldn't have been love...

She vividly remembered how he had teased her, mocked her, always under a veneer of light-hearted humour, because Jim had rarely left her side. Had it been Liam's way of trying to reach her, to probe past her prejudice and into her heart? Was that what it had all been about? Had her perception of him been completely distorted because she hadn't liked the uncontrollable surges of emotion he stirred?

He watched the doubts flit across her eyes with a grim satisfaction. Then his voice took on a harsher edge. 'And what I can't forgive you for is that you wilfully denied what we should have had together.'

'I loved Jim, Liam,' she whispered, driven to protest his claim.

'No!' He shook his head, closing his eyes in anguished denial. 'No, I don't believe that. I can't believe it.' His eyes opened to bright, accusing slits. 'You felt it that first night. A quickening of every sense. A recognition that this is the woman... this is the man! I looked at you, and no one else existed but us. It had to be the same for you!'

'No!' she choked. And yet, she had been terribly aware of him. But only because of the way he had looked at her—undressing her with hot, hungry eyes!

'Yes!' he insisted on an explosive breath. His jaw tightened and his hands ran down her throat, over her shoulders, and closed possessively around her upper arms. 'When I took you in my arms to dance, your body quivered in response to mine. You wanted me, yet you pushed away. Why, Gina?'

Because... he had excited her and she had resented his power to do that. And he was so... so blatantly sexy, the kind of man that automatically made one wonder what it might be like to be with him, and he probably excited such thoughts in every woman who ever saw him. It had stung her pride, and stirred an even fiercer loyalty to Jim, who never even looked at another woman. How could she admit to feeling attracted... physically attracted...?

'It wasn't right!' she burst out defensively.

Liam's fingers pressed bruisingly as he shook her in pent-up frustration. 'It was right! It was perfect!'

'I was with Jim!' she cried. 'He was your friend! Didn't that mean anything to you?'

'It meant you had made a mistake.' He dragged in a deep breath, as if to counter pain. 'And I wanted to kill him.' His eyes seared her with the anguish of his conflict. 'My best friend... since we were boys. And for you, I wanted to kill him.'

To Gina's enormous relief he released her and paced away, as if driven by flailing whips wielded by demons. She sank down on the nearest couch, too shaken to remain standing. If Liam had loved her... it explained so much. Why he had never come to see Jim again... and the wedding! It must have been hell for him to endure seeing her married to someone else... having to take part in the ceremony. And she had thought so meanly of him... been so wrong!

When Liam turned back to her he had re-established some control of himself. His face was carved into an austere pride, but his eyes still held a feverish glitter. His hand lifted into a clenched fist. 'Why didn't you have the courage to come away with me when I asked you, Gina?'

Guilt and compassion for all the pain she had unwittingly given him tore through her heart. Impossible to say she had judged him to be dishonourable to his friend. In his own way, he had not. Her mind sought a soft answer.

'You had a strong appeal, Liam, but there was nothing else. You never showed me anything else. There's more to love than sex, Liam.'

He shook his head. 'I would have done anything for you.'

'I'm sorry. I didn't realise...' Her eyes begged his understanding. 'I thought... you were not the kind of man I could trust with my life.'

'And Jim was,' he said with bitter irony.

'I thought so,' she sighed. But their marriage hadn't worked out the way she had expected, or wanted. Most of the time she had felt more like a mother than a wife to Jim: soothing, supporting, organising things for him.

'And how did you feel on your wedding night?'

The whiplash of the question brought a stinging heat to her cheeks. 'I don't know what you mean,' she mumbled evasively.

'Oh, yes, you do, Gina,' Liam taunted, strolling back towards her with vibrant menace in every step. 'You told me this morning that you remember what

I did on your wedding day. Impossible to forget, you said. And I agree with you. It's been quite impossible to forget the response I got when I kissed you.'

He sat on the wide armrest of the couch, looking down at her with a bitter intensity that pinned her to utter stillness, even while his fingers slowly stroked her hair. Her throat dried up. Her pulse beat so hard she was afraid Liam would see the telltale flutter in her neck. His words slid into a churning morass of emotions.

'I stood beside Jim in the church, willing you to change your mind, to say no to him when it came time to exchange your vows. She can't do it, I told myself. She must realise it's wrong. But you went through with it in a clear, steady voice. And I hated you then, Gina.'

His voice lowered to almost a whisper, but a vibrant echo of passion rang behind every word. 'But still I could not let go. You kept looking at me, Gina, flicking agitated little glances that told me you were in some turmoil of mind.'

'You were drunk, Liam. I was frightened you would spoil things,' she explained huskily.

He shook his head. 'I was beyond drunkenness. The pain couldn't be blunted by anything.'

'But that's why I kept glancing at you,' Gina insisted. 'There was no other reason.'

His eyes probed hers, challenging her assertion, mocking it. His fingers trailed across her cheek and traced the line of her lips with tantalising delicacy. 'I don't believe you, Gina,' he said softly. 'When

I kissed you, I knew then. Beyond any possible doubt. She'll come with me now, I thought. She can't deny this.'

'Stop it, Liam!' she burst out, unable to bear the teasing touch and tormented beyond endurance by his version of what had happened. She remembered the shock she had felt at the sensations he had aroused with his kiss. The shock of realisation that he really was exciting her, drawing her into... A terrible panic had coursed through her. She had hated him for making her feel things that she knew should only be felt with her husband. And she had hit out in horror at her own weakness!

'You shouldn't have done it!' she whispered in confused anguish. 'I was Jim's wife!'

A grim ferocity tightened his face and exploded into voice. 'It still wasn't too late! Unconsummated marriages can be annulled. You could have...'

'No! I could never have done that!' she cried, appalled that he would even consider such a course. 'The hurt to Jim...the pain...the agony of having the two people he loved...'

'Do you think I didn't know it? That it wasn't tearing me apart?' he retorted hoarsely. His grimace was a bitter acknowledgement. 'I did realise later that it was impossible...for you, Gina. Much, much later, when everything was far too late.'

She shook her head. 'I didn't want you, Liam.' And she hadn't! Not the reckless, driving, devil-may-care man he had seemed to be.

His eyes condemned her. 'You did, damn you! Even if it was only sexually. And I hope you felt as cheated as I did on your wedding night!'

He whirled off the armrest and stalked away from her, putting the next couch between them before he turned and gripped its back support with spread arms, leaning forward to hurl his words at her, his face dark with the violence of his emotions.

'I hope when Jim kissed you, you yearned for the intensity of feeling that my mouth stirred in yours. I hope when your bodies came together, you remembered how mine felt. I hope...'

'Stop it! Stop it!' Gina was on her feet, screaming at him, her heart pumping a violent protest at the havoc he was wreaking inside her. 'How dare you...?'

'Oh, I dare, Gina!' His teeth flashed menacingly at her. 'I dare anything!'

He straightened up and threw a careless gesture around the room. 'That's why I can afford anything I want now. You see, Gina, I didn't care what happened to me in the years after you became Jim's wife! I flirted with death a thousand times. Without you, I didn't have any desire to live.'

He turned his back on her and paced away, talking in a rough staccato that jabbed images into Gina's brain, replacing all her preconceived ideas about him and his feelings for her. She listened in a kind of spongy daze, as if she herself was being reshaped by the passion pouring from his tongue.

'I've done things that I'm proud of, but a lot more of which I'm not. Gun-running to South

America, arms dealing, getting refugees out. Anything and everything. In those days, I didn't care. They called me the mad Irish Aussie, and I earned the reputation of daring anything. And doing it.

'I demanded the most outrageous fees and commissions, always expecting that my death would save them from paying out. What did I care? Other men around me were killed. Time after time. But I seemed to bear a charmed life.'

He gave a harsh laugh and shook his head. 'Once we sailed a boat-load of rich refugees out of Kampuchea. It was dead of night and a wild monsoon blew up. The mainsail snapped from the mast and someone had to go up and fix it. Sixty feet up in a howling wind. And your face went with me, Gina.'

He turned and stared at her, his eyes slightly unfocused, remembering. 'I clung to that mast, riding the wind, and you were there...'

He laughed again in bitter derision. 'They thought I was a hero. A hero, when I was actually courting death! So they paid me well for saving them. And I went on accumulating money.'

His eyes sharpened, deliberately dismissing her as he resumed pacing. 'But eventually the madness left me. I could shut the memory of you out of my mind for some of the time. And the power and privileges of wealth beckoned. I turned my back on physical danger and became immersed in the mental stimulation of playing with the world's bankers. And in a way, that worked better, Gina.' He flashed her a searing look. 'I got over you.'

Gina's heart felt an odd wrench. The riveting passion of Liam's story had swept away all her defensive prejudices... her entrenched hostility towards him. The terrible depth of his despair, caused by the emotions he had felt when she had married Jim, had almost moved her to tears. She wanted to reach out to him, but if all his feeling for her had gone...

'Then why today, Liam?' she asked softly. 'When you saw me through the doorway, why didn't you just pass me by?'

He halted, and it seemed he consciously relaxed his face into a sardonic little smile. But there was no smile in his eyes. They glittered over her with something akin to antipathy.

'I couldn't.' Self-contempt coated the words. 'Even after all these years, I couldn't turn away.'

She had wanted to turn away from him, and been unable to. She understood that now. She wondered what would have happened if she had not already been engaged to Jim before he'd introduced her to Liam; whether she could have resisted Liam's strong physical attraction if there had been no sense of betrayal forcing her to keep her distance.

Certainly, it had never been given a fair chance. Her relationship with Jim had coloured her reaction to every man. After his years in the orphanage, Jim had desperately needed the emotional security of her commitment. In contrast, Liam had not seemed to need anybody to support him in any way. Yet he and Jim had shared the same background. And she had been so wrong about so many things.

She looked up at him, saw the bitter pride on his face, and sighed for a past that could not be replayed any differently now. 'What fate dictated that you should walk down that corridor and see me at my desk?' she asked.

'Fate?' He rolled the word off his tongue with a kind of whimsical derision, and Gina didn't know if he was mocking her or himself.

For a moment, she wondered if there had been no chance involved at all, that he had known she was there and had deliberately sought her out. But then he shook his head and offered her an ironic smile as he answered her question.

'I had an appointment with an accountant on the floor above yours. I must have pressed the wrong button in the elevator. When I realised my mistake I decided to take the stairs. I happened to glance into your office as I walked past. And there you were. The phantom of all my old dreams. In the flesh.'

Liam gave Gina no time to consider the enormity of the coincidence. He walked towards her, his smile twisting as his words gathered a spine-tingling intensity.

'I said to myself . . . I'll prove I'm over her. She's just a face from the past now. A finished part of my life. I meant to pass the time of day for a few moments, and then move on.'

His arm suddenly snaked around her waist and pulled her hard against him. 'Damn your fascination!'

Gina was so surprised by his action that she did not immediately fight it. Her startled eyes flew up to his and were briefly caught in a swirl of heady, intoxicating emotion. She quickly dropped her eyelashes, but already the urge...the need to stay where she was and savour the feelings he provoked was almost too tempting to deny.

She was deeply jolted by such thoughts. In the two years since Jim's death she had been completely numb to any sexual attraction, automatically rejecting even the slightest physical advance made on her, and the occasional attempt at flirtation. She was not interested in casual encounters anyway, and her marriage had not been so perfect that she wanted to rush into another involvement. Besides, first and foremost came her commitment to Debbie's welfare. She didn't have time for dalliances.

Yet she could not rid herself of the fascination of knowing more of Liam...what he felt. With a tactile pleasure that stirred even more uneasy thoughts, she slid her hands up to his shoulders. She told herself she would push away from him as soon as it became practicable.

'You said it was over, Liam,' she reminded him, her eyes darting up to catch any revealing expression.

His gaze roved hungrily over her upturned face. 'I don't love you any more, Gina. What a fool I was to feel the way... I can live without you...'

His voice was hoarse, abrupt, discordant... was he telling the truth?

'But it's not finished.' His teeth clenched over the words. 'I still want you, more than I've ever wanted any woman. And I've got to get you out of my system. Otherwise you'll eat away at me, destroying me in the same way as a raging sea destroys a sandy shore. It's like an ache that's never been appeased, and I don't intend to live with that ache any longer. I have to have you. And I'm going to.'

His other arm had come around her, pressing her closer, moulding her lower body to his. 'You feel the same, Gina. Don't lie. You can't hold Jim between us now. And I intend to kiss you senseless. To own and possess...'

'Liam, please...' she begged, frightened by his intensity. Admitting a fascination with fire was one thing, but not when it threatened to burst into a conflagration that couldn't be controlled. She dropped her hands to his chest and strained away. 'Not like this...'

'I can feel your thighs quivering against mine. There's an ache of wanting spreading through your belly. Nerves leaping in excitement. There's never been anything like this before in your life. Tell me it's so, Gina. Speak the truth!'

He rained passionate kisses on her face as she tried to twist away from him.

'Admit it, damn you! Admit it!' he breathed in tortured gasps.

'No!' she cried, even as the weakness he was so accurately describing attacked her resistance further—her lips parting to receive his, her breasts swollen and tense as they brushed against his chest, and her thighs were quivering...

'You want me as much as I want you.'

'No!' she sobbed.

'Then prove it. Open your mouth. Show me that I can't arouse a desire to match mine. Prove it to me.'

'I . . .'

He denied her an answer, his lips stealing it from her. And Gina gave up the struggle, seduced by the need that clamoured through her, demanding that she savour the sensations Liam evoked with his passionate sensuality.

Her arms wound around his neck and she returned his kiss, flinging all inhibitions aside in a wild search for the truth. The erotic interplay of their mouths swiftly developed an intimate intensity that completely shook Gina's previous conception of how exciting lovemaking could be.

She had never had any other lover but Jim, and he had always been gentle, anxious for her pleasure; a warmly caring man who had neither evoked nor shown any inclination for wild passion.

Jim had curled around her soul.

Liam clawed at it, demanding entry.

And yes, she wanted him. She wanted Liam Shannon, wanted to feel him deep inside her, wanted him in every way... wanted him as she had never wanted Jim, despite the love she had shared with him. This had nothing to do with love. She knew it, yet the desire Liam aroused was beyond her control.

Her body melted with a purely wanton pleasure to the stirring hardness of Liam's against her, and her need to take him was dreadfully compelling. Submission had nothing to do with it. She felt as violently aggressive as he; wanting to possess as he would possess; reaching to the core of him; taking, taking all the satisfaction that had somehow eluded her in her marriage.

It was wicked madness, and while Liam kept kissing her Gina gloried in it, uncaring of anything but gleaning the utmost excitement out of every moment. His lips pressed his seal of possession along her throat, over her face, on her lips, driving towards the union they both wanted. And, even when he tore his mouth from hers to drag in breath, she exulted in the quick heave of his chest against her breasts. His arms tightened around her, crushing her even closer. His mouth swept across her hair, fanning it with warmth.

'Say you want me, Gina,' he coaxed softly.

'Yes...' The word dragged out on a ragged breath: an admission, a surrender. She didn't even think beyond her acceptance that it was the undeniable truth.

'So finally we come to it,' Liam murmured on a deep expulsion of breath.

He slowly eased his embrace, his hands dragging up her body to gently cup her face. His eyes drank in the glazed wonder in hers, and he smiled . . . a joyous, triumphant smile.

'How long I've waited to see you look at me like this!' he said, and he could not keep the exultation from his voice. 'Nights I've dreamed of it. Days I've dreamed of it. Now, at last . . . I'm going to make love to you all afternoon. For the next twenty-four hours. All my life.'

His arms wrapped around her and he laughed, a wild, excited laughter that tore along Gina's stretched nerves and blew sanity back into her mind.

She couldn't stay with Liam. She had to get home to Debbie. Her daughter needed all of her time for as long as it took to give her the only chance there was of restoring her eyesight. She wasn't free to do as she liked, and if she faced the truth of this situation with Liam, she didn't like it, anyway.

He had told her quite bluntly that all he wanted was to work her out of his system.

And however much her body ached to be indulged with the pleasure he would give her, that was all it was . . . pleasure.

And to have it meant a total capitulation of all the principles she had always lived by.

Liam grabbed her hand and pulled her towards the doors at the far end of the room. 'We'll be more comfortable in the state-room, my darling,' he said persuasively.

Gina weakened under the strong attraction that drew her along with him. Why couldn't she indulge herself this once? she argued. It was so tempting. She couldn't stay all night, but a few hours ... even the afternoon wouldn't matter. She had made so many sacrifices for Debbie's sake, surely she could forgive herself this one selfishness. If she went to bed with Liam, maybe it would resolve the terrible tension that had always been between them.

Or make it worse.

And she couldn't trust Liam to let her go when ... afterwards ... if once wasn't enough to rid him of his obsessive desire for her. He wanted everything on his terms, and she couldn't accept them. It was madness to succumb, like playing Russian roulette, with a man who only a few hours ago she had thought she hated! She had to get out of it.

The impossibility of Liam accepting her change of heart almost paralysed her mind. Liam wasn't about to take another rejection! Not after she had shown how vulnerable she was to his compelling sexuality. God! War, he had called it! She needed all her wits to win this battle of wills!

He opened the door and waved her to precede him into a plush bedroom: walls of panelled oak, and a king-size bed covered with quilted silk and massed pillows, promising soft, sensual comfort...

Gina hung back, a conflict of interests raging through her. 'Liam, please...a moment...' She tried to work some saliva into her arid mouth. 'I ... I have to go to the bathroom. Is there one close by?'

His eyes sprang at hers, questioning. What he saw apparently satisfied him. He nodded back to the end of the entertainment-room. 'The door by the stairs.'

'Thank you.' She forced a smile. 'Why not collect a bottle of champagne and some glasses? I . . . I feel nervous with you. It can only...help... Oh! I need something that will help me feel more relaxed . . .'

He looked at her quizzically for a moment, then grinned. His whole face lit with elation. 'If that's what you want. And to take our time! Yes! You're absolutely right. Something to celebrate.'

Gina felt a wrenching regret for what she was about to do, but no good purpose could be served by staying. Liam didn't love her. And she didn't love him. The revelation of his former feeling for her had stunned and touched her deeply, but she didn't owe him anything. She never had.

He watched her walk down the room to the door he had indicated. She glanced back at him as she opened it. He took a bottle of champagne from the bar and collected two glasses from a rack behind it. He lifted them to her in exultant salute before turning away and going back into the state-room.

Feeling desperately guilty, despite all her reasoning, Gina raced up the stairs and across the deck to where the outboard motor-boat had been tied. For several heart-pounding moments, her fingers fumbled over the way the rope had been fastened. No one tried to stop her. A wave brought the outboard in closer, easing the tension on the knot enough for her to work it free. She hurtled down the ladder to the boat.

To her dizzying relief, Liam had left the key in the ignition. She switched on the motor, thrust the gear-lever one way, and sat down with a thump when the boat took off in reverse. She heard shouts from the yacht, but she didn't look up. She wrestled with the controls until she worked out how to manage them, then headed for the marina.

Liam would hate her, she thought, and in a way she hated herself for running away from him. But Debbie was waiting at home for her. Debbie...going blind. She couldn't have afforded the physical and emotional toll that Liam would have drawn from her. She couldn't afford any distraction. Not until she had done all she could for her daughter.

CHAPTER FOUR

SHEER exhaustion compounded the bitter frustration that dogged Gina's footsteps all the way home to Esme's narrow little terrace house in Paddington. In the excitement of her escape she had left her handbag behind on Liam's yacht. But she couldn't have gone back for it, couldn't have faced him, even though he was sure to find it...and her wallet, which contained her address.

Tears trickled down her cheeks as she tottered to the front door. Her doorkey had been in her handbag, and she had to ring the bell for Esme to come and let her inside. She leaned against the porch wall, so emotionally and physically drained that she could not summon the will to stop crying.

Esme opened the door and exclaimed her surprise and concern at seeing her in such distress. 'What's wrong?' she asked kindly.

It was too much for Gina. The tears fell even faster as she poured out all the wrongs. 'I've lost my job. And my handbag as well. Which had my severance cheque in it, and I had no money for a bus so I had to walk home. And I fell over and laddered my stockings. And I'll have to find another job and...and...'

Esme wrapped a comforting arm around Gina's shoulders and quickly drew her inside, clucking in such a motherly way that Gina ended up sobbing on her huge, cushiony bosom.

'It's not the end of the world,' Esme soothed, stroking her hair and patting her on the back. 'I'm going to sell a painting. Working on it right now. We'll get Debbie's eyes fixed up, don't you worry. You've been pushing yourself too hard, Gina. What you need is a good long sleep.'

'Yes,' Gina sniffed, trying to pull herself together. She simply couldn't afford to fall apart. It would be letting her daughter down, particularly when time was such an relentless enemy. She dragged herself back under control, raised her head from Esme's ample chest and wiped her cheeks with the back of her hand. 'Sorry for collapsing on you, Esme. Where's Debbie?'

'Having her afternoon nap. Now you go right on upstairs and have a nap yourself. Forget about your job. There's always another one, and it'll do you good to have a few days off.'

'Yes,' Gina agreed wearily. 'Thanks, Esme.' She felt quite faint as she started up the staircase, and she had to clutch the banister tightly to steady herself.

'I'll show you my painting when you come back down. I've started on a completely new style,' Esme boasted with a huge, happy grin, custom-designed to cheer anyone within its radius. She burbled on with irrepressible excitement. 'When Debbie and I went shopping this morning I was describing things to her and relating the colours to feelings, and suddenly I got this great inspiration. Then we worked out a fantastic picture on the way home. Pure genius!'

Gina managed a watery smile. 'I'm looking forward to seeing it.' But it was a problem to find words that sounded like praise, while still being honest in her comments on Esme's paintings.

Very quietly Gina closed the bedroom door behind her and leaned against it as she slid off her shoes. Debbie was fast asleep in the twin bed across from hers. Gina knew she shouldn't risk waking her, but she couldn't resist the impulse to climb into bed with her daughter and cuddle the child to her heart. She needed to hold her, needed love to fill the gnawing emptiness that Liam's sexual impact had left inside her.

Very gently she lifted the bedclothes and carefully insinuated herself around the soft, small body of her child. She slid an arm under the pillow and rested her head beside Debbie's, breathing in the clean, wholesome scent of baby shampoo that clung to the bob of black curls.

Debbie stirred and reached out to her. 'Mummy?'

'Yes, darling,' Gina whispered, a huge lump welling in her throat as Debbie snuggled closer to her and sighed contentedly.

Gina sighed, too. This was where she belonged, not in bed with Liam, satisfying some purely physical instincts. A wave of strong maternal love washed away any lingering regret for the decision she had made. Yet, as she closed her eyes and drifted towards sleep, the memory of Liam telling her of his love niggled at her mind. If only she had known... but it was too late now, she thought sadly. It had been too late when she had first met Liam. Always too late...

Gina felt totally disorientated when she awoke. The time felt wrong; she was in Debbie's bed; dressed in her work clothes! She groaned as memory flooded back. Liam Shannon! Would he come after her, or leave well enough alone? The problem raised such a welter of confusing emotions that Gina hurriedly pushed it aside.

A quick check of her watch showed that it was almost five o'clock. The company might call her for a job tonight. She had to get on with her own life, earning all the money she could for Debbie's operation.

Gina pushed herself out of bed, stripped off her crumpled clothes, grabbed her housecoat and headed for the bathroom. The revitalising sting of the shower-spray washed away the dull-witted hangover from her afternoon sleep. She pulled a brush through her hair and hurried downstairs, her stomach grumbling for food.

She stopped dead in the kitchen doorway, her gaze caught and held by the painting on Esme's easel.

It was like nothing she had ever done before. This was primitive magic—all bold strokes and rampant colour, depicting a wildly improbable garden from which poked the faces of the most extraordinary animals, all happily grinning as if they were playing an amusing game of hide and seek.

Esme had Debbie in her arms, pointing out all the facets of the picture, as if the child could really see them. 'And here's the giraffe. See his long neck stretching out from behind the tree? I gave him curly eyelashes just like yours...'

Debbie was staring at the painting, absolutely enthralled by all Esme told her. 'What colour did you do that?' Debbie asked.

'A very friendly yellow. Like the feeling when you're happy.' Esme tickled her and she giggled.

Gina moved quietly up behind them, enthralled and enraptured by the giant step Esme had made in her work. For once she could speak the truth plainly as she saw it, and the pleasure of being able to do so bounced around her heart.

'You are a genius, Esme,' she said softly, and her warm appreciation covered all her friend's qualities: the wonderful manner she had with Debbie, the sympathetic support she gave them both, and the imaginative artistry that had produced such a marvellous painting.

Esme turned, her face glowing with exultant happiness. She rubbed her cheek against Debbie's. 'We did it together, didn't we, love?'

'It's our secret garden, Mummy,' Debbie agreed, beaming with pleasure.

'It's pure magic!' Gina declared with honest conviction.

Esme gave her rollicking laugh that defied the world to beat her if it could. 'This we will sell!' she proclaimed with ringing certainty. She turned back to the painting, a furrow of concern crossing her face. 'I don't know for how much, but it will sell.'

Debbie wriggled down to run over to Gina. 'It's the best Esme's ever done, Mummy,' she crowed excitedly.

Gina hoisted her up high, to Debbie's squealing delight. 'It sure is!' she agreed, and gave her daughter a big bear-hug.

'And that's not all!' Esme boomed in triumph. She swooped over to the kitchen table and held Gina's handbag aloft. 'Found and returned! You're not going to believe this, Gina,' she burbled on, 'but the most dreadfully handsome man you've ever seen came to our door with it while you were asleep.'

Gina's heart did a double-flip. 'What time?' she asked, agitated at the thought of what might have happened if she had answered the door.

'Oh, some time between three and four,' Esme said airily, then started acting out the scene with her usual relish for the dramatic and extraordinary. 'I presented myself with my most welcoming aplomb. He seemed surprised—perhaps startled is the word. I sometimes have that effect on people.'

'What did he say?' Gina asked anxiously.

'I'm getting to it,' Esme protested. ' "Does Gina York live here?" he asked. "Yes," I said. "May I see her?" he asked. "I wish to return her handbag." "Oh, you marvellous man," I said, wanting to hug him for being so kind. And gorgeous! He was actually tall enough to look me in the eye. Not many men can do that.'

'He—er—didn't mind not seeing me?' Gina asked cautiously.

Esme recollected herself. 'He frowned a bit. But I explained how terribly distressed you were when you arrived home, and that you were asleep and I didn't want to disturb you because you were utterly exhausted. So he asked me to give you the handbag and then took his leave.'

'He didn't say anything else?'

Esme heaved a regretful sigh. 'No, he was off before I could quiz him about such pertinent details as who he was, and would he like to buy a painting.'

Gina didn't know if she was relieved or disappointed. However, she did know that she didn't want to discuss Liam Shannon with Esme. She pasted a bright smile on her face.

'Well, thank heaven I got my handbag back! I guess you can be lucky sometimes, Esme. I'm going to make myself a couple of sandwiches to celebrate. I'm absolutely starving.'

Since food was a subject dear to Esme's heart, the issue of the handbag was immediately dropped. Gina had just wolfed down her sandwiches when the company telephoned her.

Mr Vincente, the art dealer, was still having trouble with the Australian accent and finding his way around Sydney. He would feel a lot more confident and would appreciate it very much if Gina could look after him again tonight. He wanted to dine at a good Italian restaurant. Was she available? Mr Vincente had specifically asked for her.

Gina smiled, remembering the fifty-dollar tip he had given her last night. The poor man was obviously very lonely, which just went to prove that wealth wasn't everything. Although Gina wouldn't mind having some of it for Debbie.

She quickly agreed to the assignment and jotted down the details. She was to meet him at eight o'clock at the Regent Hotel. The company had nominated Lucio's as the best choice of Italian restaurants for Mr Vincente. A taxi would be sent to collect her at seven forty-five.

Gina sighed over the fact that she had just blunted her appetite, and then she remembered that Mr Vincente's business was in art evaluation. She wondered if she dared ask him to look at Esme's painting. It probably wasn't very ethical when one part of her job was to make sure he wasn't harassed in what was, to him, a foreign country, but...maybe she could lead into it quite naturally if he was here in Australia to look at local art.

The doorbell rang just as she put the telephone down, and Gina tensed, wondering if Liam had decided to come back. Esme bustled out to answer the summons, and Gina breathed more easily when the caller's voice was distinctly female. Only a few moments later she heard the door being shut. Esme reappeared, bearing a sheaf of magnificent red roses.

'They're for you, Gina,' she declared with beaming pleasure.

'They can't be!' Gina protested, yet even as she denied the gift her mind flew to Liam. But why would he send her red roses? 'Is there a card?' she asked, incredulity giving way to curiosity.

Esme laid the sheaf on the table and stripped off the cellophane. 'None that I can see.'

And there wasn't one. Just twelve perfect blooms. Esme had a lovely time raising all sorts of romantic questions as she arranged the roses in a vase, while Gina kept insisting it had to be a mistake of some kind. Debbie said they smelled beautiful, and Esme broke off a velvet-soft petal for her to press to her nose.

The gift certainly gave them pleasure, Gina thought ruefully, but what could Liam mean by it? It had to be Liam. No one else of Gina's acquaintance would make such an extravagant gesture. If it wasn't a mistake.

The question exercised her mind while she helped Debbie with her evening meal, bathed her and dressed her in her pyjamas. Red roses were for love, but Liam didn't love her any more. Maybe he thought that seduction was a surer way of getting what he wanted than the direct confrontation he had tried today. If he had sent those flowers, he was giving her one clear message...he didn't intend to leave her alone.

And how was she going to cope with that? The question was even thornier than the roses. Would Liam ever take no for an answer? Maybe she was conjuring up problems that might not eventuate. Perhaps the gift was an ironic way of saying goodbye to a love that had never really been, and was now completely dead.

And why did that thought depress her? Hadn't she decided that she couldn't afford a complication like Liam Shannon in her life? Feeling hopelessly at odds with herself, Gina took Debbie downstairs to Esme, then returned to her bedroom to get ready for her evening assignment.

In reaction against the emotional turmoil of the day, Gina chose her red crêpe dress. Somehow, the bold colour was a statement of self-assertiveness. Certainly not wishy-washy. The style was demure enough to be perfectly respectable: high-necked and hugging her figure to the hipline, which featured a low tie-sash before the skirt broke into a swirl of knife pleats.

Gina applied a more vivid make-up than usual, tempted to prove to herself that she could still look as good as she had when she'd married Jim. She didn't stop to wonder why that should be important to her tonight. She just needed to feel good about herself. She slid high-heeled red sandals on to her feet, and had just finished varnishing her nails when Esme called out that the taxi had arrived.

That was one good thing about this job, Gina thought approvingly. The company was meticulous about providing transport. She raced downstairs, kissed Debbie goodnight and was off.

The drive from Paddington into the city was very fast. All the traffic lights went their way, and Gina arrived at the hotel with almost ten minutes to spare. Still, it could have gone the other way, and the company was a stickler for punctuality.

The Regent Hotel was one of the most prestigious hotels in Sydney—indeed, in all the world. Towering above Circular Quay, it commanded magnificent views of the harbour. The few times Gina had been there to collect clients, she had been awed by the sheer size of the lobby, which rose three podium levels high, creating a wonderfully extravagant sense of spaciousness. A centrepiece of small trees flourished under a bank of skylights, and planter boxes around the balconies softened the dramatic lines of the architecture. A huge winding staircase of South Australian granite and brass railings descended to one side of the trees. Behind them was the Lobby Restaurant, set out like a pavement-styled café. Above was a mezzanine floor containing a coffee bar and a more luxurious restaurant.

Gina checked her watch as she entered the hotel. She was still eight minutes early for her appointment. Just in front of her was a grouping of deep leather lounges, and she decided to sit down and bide her time watching the coming and going of the expensively dressed patrons of the hotel.

'Gina!'

Her head snapped around.

Liam!

He rose from one of the armchairs that faced away from the hotel entrance. The surprise she had caught on his face was swiftly erased as his eyes flashed over her in comprehensive appraisal. His face tightened, and the vivid blue eyes were strangely opaque when they lifted to hers.

Every nerve in Gina's body was leaping with apprehension. Liam Shannon had already lost her one job today. If he forced another confrontation now...made a scene...but what else could she do but stand her ground?

His mouth twisted. 'Relax, Gina. The war is over. I surrender. The spoils are yours. I sue for peace!'

Her mind couldn't accept what he was saying. The words bounced around her head, but they had no relevance when applied to the man standing in front of her. 'What are you doing here, Liam?' she demanded, her voice high and strained.

How could she be cursed with two coincidental meetings with him in the one day? Unless...had he lied about taking the elevator to the wrong floor this morning? There had been that funny pause before he agreed he had seen her by pure chance. But he couldn't have known she would come here tonight. That was certainly beyond the realms of possibility.

He shrugged, as if the question was of no consequence. 'I have a suite of rooms here for my convenience. At the moment I'm waiting for a business contact to meet me. We're going out to dinner.'

His matter-of-fact tone took the sharp edge off her tension. Liam was wealthy. He would naturally gravitate to a hotel such as this. It was sheer bad luck that he happened to be in the lobby when she had entered.

But still Gina could not relax. 'You...gave me the impression you were free this evening,' she said suspiciously, not understanding this extraordinary change of manner to her, and fearfully questioning if she could trust him not to make more trouble for her.

'I would have been. For you,' he answered softly.

Gina's heart contracted. If she had not run away... The memory of the passion he had ignited with his kiss sent a rush of heat around her body. Her skin tingled with a flushed awareness of the response he could so easily arouse. She dropped her eyes, all too conscious that they might reflect her vulnerability. Her mind skittered over all the reasons why she could not allow herself to become involved with Liam Shannon, then clutched desperately at her most immediate line of defence.

'I have an appointment,' she said, her eyes flicking up in defiant challenge.

His face perceptibly tightened, but he held her gaze steadily and answered her without any trace of animosity. 'So you told me. This morning.' He paused a moment, his eyes searching hers with compelling intensity. 'I hope your *lover* appreciates you... as much as I would.'

Gina stared back at him in utter incredulity, then remembered the excuse she had given him this morning in Mr Jepherson's office. She had forgotten all about it but, on its recall, Gina was even more stunned that Liam was exercising such civilised restraint after the explosive violence of this afternoon. Given his understanding of the situation... She inwardly writhed at the false impression she had unwittingly created.

'I don't have a lover,' she blurted out, then flushed with embarrassment at the involuntary admission. 'I . . . I lied to you. It seemed the only way to . . . to . . .'

'To get rid of me,' he finished for her, then dragged in a deep breath and expelled it in a long sigh. 'I thought . . . Oh, never mind what I thought.'

He smiled, a dazzlingly happy smile that caught the breath in Gina's throat. Her mind couldn't grasp what was going on in his, but she was fascinated by the change in him. She sensed no aggression at all. This was an entirely new Liam Shannon, and he was overwhelmingly attractive.

He took her hand. A quiver ran down Gina's arm at his gentle touch. Liam's eyes held hers, projecting a warm reassurance.

'I don't want to hurt you, Gina. Please believe that. I don't blame you for running away from me this afternoon. I wanted too much . . . too soon.'

'Liam . . .' Her throat was impossibly dry. Her mind screamed that 'too soon' only meant that he was prepared to take more time in getting her into his bed. Nothing had really changed. She withdrew her hand from his, nursing it gingerly, as though it had been burned. She swallowed hard. 'I know I said . . . I wanted you, but I can't give you what you want, Liam. The kind of affair you have in mind doesn't fit into my life.'

'I realise that,' he said softly, confounding her anew with his understanding.

Or was it a ploy to get under her guard? Her eyes wildly searched the sincerity in his, wanting to believe that he genuinely cared about her feelings. 'Why did you send the roses?' she asked, and it felt as if her whole being was poised on a knife's edge, waiting for his answer.

It seemed an eternity in coming, and she sensed he was carefully weighing his words before he spoke. 'I want another chance. To start all over again, Gina. From scratch.' His mouth curved in wry appeal. 'Boy meets girl?'

Did he really mean that? The proposition had a compelling attraction, but even as she considered it ... yearned for the possibility ... she knew it was an impossible dream. Reality held the shadows of too much pain in the past. Gina felt ravaged by a multitude of regrets as she spoke the hopeless truth.

'We can't go back. Too much has happened. To you and to me, Liam.'

'What's gone is gone,' he said with quiet emphasis, and the determined purpose in his eyes wiped out the past. 'I aim on having a long future. Consider sharing it with me, Gina. Give it a chance. That's all I ask.'

She wanted to! Her whole being cried to give in to the temptation he was offering, but she wasn't completely free, and never would be completely free of the past. Would Liam want Debbie? She was Jim's daughter. And just as he had hated her for loving Jim, he might hate her daughter, and herself for putting Debbie first. Because she had to do precisely that. At least until after the operation. And if Debbie didn't recover her eyesight ...

'There are problems, Liam,' she answered honestly. 'I'm not sure... I need some time to think about it.' Time! The word reminded her of Mr Vincente. She glanced agitatedly at her watch. It was five past eight. 'I have to go!'

'Wait!' His hand reached out to her.

'No!' She backed away. 'I really can't! Please, Liam... I've got a job to do and I'm already late. I'll talk to you tomorrow. It can't be any other way.'

She turned to find Mr Vincente bearing down on her. His arms spread wide with welcoming pleasure. 'Gina, my dear.' He grasped her hand in both of his and shook it warmly. 'I am so glad that you could accommodate me again tonight.'

'I'm sorry for keeping you waiting, Mr Vincente,' Gina apologised, burningly aware of Liam just behind her.

'A trifle!' The rotund Italian beamed over her shoulder. 'I see you have an eye for beauty, Mr Shannon.'

'I appreciate a lot of things, Vincente,' Liam drawled, his voice scraping through Gina's ears with the edge of a serrated knife. It was obvious to Gina that he didn't appreciate their conversation having been cut short.

The comment won a pleased chuckle from the Italian who took Gina's elbow and turned her to face Liam. 'Mr Shannon is joining us for dinner tonight, Gina.'

Her heart sank. Of all the men who could have been Liam's business contact, why did it have to be Mr Vincente? Everything within her shrank from the idea of sitting across from Liam at a dinner table and being forced into making small-talk when there was so much left unresolved between them.

Reluctantly and wretchedly she met Liam's eyes, and knew he hated the situation, too. A seething cauldron of immeasurable emotions looked back at her. She sensed the superhuman control he exerted to pull himself up, to accept the unacceptable. His eyes clouded into the same glassy, opaque look that had shuttered his thoughts when he had spoken of her supposed lover.

'The lady and I have met before,' he said, a rough edge to each deliberately spoken word, straining to filter all feeling from his speech, but not quite succeeding. 'In fact, we were just talking over old times, weren't we, Gina?'

'Yes,' she agreed with a false brightness that endeavoured to cover her own inner turmoil.

The Italian patted her hand. 'Well, Gina and I got to know each other very well last night. You always seem to have a beautiful woman on your arm, Mr Shannon. I thought tonight I might turn the tables on you. Make you a little jealous of me. No?'

'Oh, yes!' Liam agreed, his eyes narrowed to hard slits. 'I'm extremely jealous. So jealous, that I doubt I can talk business with you tonight. Or any night, Vincente. Never again. Unless . . .'

He paused, his gaze fixed relentlessly on the sudden stiffening of alarm which had snuffed out the happy humour on Mr Vincente's face. The ultimatum was delivered with deadly incisiveness.

'Unless you do me the favour of leaving the lady with me for the evening.'

His ruthless undercutting of the situation startled Gina into protest. 'Liam, please...'

He ignored her. 'Well, Vincente? Make your decision! What do you want? What is more important to you?'

The Italian threw up his hands and spluttered into speech. 'What can I say? Gina is not mine to give! The company that arranges transport and interpreters and helps with business connections... Gina does me a favour. That is all.'

'You won't lose by it, Vincente. And neither will she. Get someone else, if you like. I'll foot the bill. But Gina is mine.'

The poor, confused man turned to Gina in supplication, his accent thickening in his distress. 'I call the night off, eh? It is no good.'

'I'm sorry, Mr Vincente,' Gina said with genuine sympathy for his plight.

'An unfortunate mistake.' He flicked an appeasing look at Liam. 'You will call me tomorrow? On the progress?'

'You have my word,' Liam replied coldly.

Mr Vincente darted away like a fish that had slithered off a particularly nasty hook.

Gina turned reproachful eyes to Liam. 'That was mean and unkind.'

His mouth tightened and his eyes were so hard they could have cut steel. 'You wanted to be with him?'

In all honesty, she could not argue that. 'Not particularly,' she sighed. 'But I do need the money. I've already lost one job today because of you, and . . .'

'Money!' He breathed the word as though he despised it. 'I'll pay you well, Gina. More than you'd get from him. So let's not waste any more time.'

He took her arm and steered her towards the bank of elevators. His impatience with her scraped over Gina's sensibilities. Although she understood Liam's frustration with the situation Mr Vincente had presented, she was not at all sure she liked the way he had dealt with it . . . cutting the poor old man dead and giving her no choice in the matter.

He was riding roughshod over her, just as he had done this morning. And now she would never get a chance to talk to Mr Vincente about Esme's painting. Liam was altogether too single-minded. And high-handed!

Yet there was more to be resolved than the sorting out of their personal differences. Gina was convinced now that Liam did have the money to help her with Debbie, but she could hardly approach the matter until a better understanding had been reached between them. Caution dictated that such a delicate matter be left to another time.

Possibly the best thing to do would be to make an arrangement to see him tomorrow, and ask for a loan which she could pay back on terms which were within her capabilities. If he really cared about her, surely he would be sympathetic to the urgency of Debbie's problem?

Some people walked out of an elevator just as they reached it, and Gina stepped into the compartment with Liam, silently determining to be tactful, but also feeling it was very necessary to set him straight on a few ground rules if there was to be any future for them.

'If you're taking me to your suite, Liam, I want to make it clear that it's only for talking,' she said warily.

He gave her a strangely grim smile. 'Oh, I think we can do better than that, Gina. I'm sure I can meet whatever price you put on yourself.'

There was something in his tone that made her flesh crawl. She frowned at him. 'Money might not be important to you any more, Liam, but...'

'Don't worry, Gina. If you perform really well, I'll even double your fee. I must thank Vincente tomorrow for showing me what the problem was,' he continued, and suddenly his eyes were glittering with hatred. 'I might have stayed blind long enough to propose marriage to you. What a fool I would have been!'

Perform...for a fee...the price she put on herself! Suddenly the words all whirled into a horrible pattern that knocked Gina speechless. How could he think that she had come here to...to service the tubby old man who... Her mind jammed in horror. It was such a staggering misconception of her job, and her mention of money, that she was too shocked to co-ordinate any thought or action.

The elevator decelerated and slid to a halt. Liam dragged her out of it while Gina was still trying to reason her way out of such a terrible impasse. He pulled a doorkey out of his pocket as he hauled her down a corridor. She wanted to scream at him, yet to deny what he seemed to be suggesting was to put into words the unspeakable, and her whole being cringed from it. She wanted to think she had misunderstood him. She must have got it wrong; Liam must have meant something else. Anything, but not that!

He jammed the key into a door and Gina found herself thrust into a luxurious corner suite. A wide entrance hallway led to a dining-suite which faced on to a spacious lounging area featuring leather sofas and potted palms. The suite obviously enjoyed a fabulous view from the huge corner windows which faced north and east, but the curtains were closed. Gina caught a glimpse of the king-size bed around the corner from the sitting-room, and a frisson of fear ran down her spine as Liam slammed the door behind them.

She stood rooted to the spot, pain needling its way through her shock, forcing her to face the inescapable. Dazedly she watched him get out a whisky bottle and splash some into a glass.

He flashed her a venomous glance. 'Don't be coy. Treat me as just another client.'

'You're mad!' Gina whispered.

'I don't usually patronise whores!' he agreed savagely. 'Not even high-class call-girls. But for you, I'll make an exception! For you, I'll always make an exception!'

The blood suddenly drained from his face, and with an inarticulate cry he hurled the glass of whisky against the wall. 'Why?' His groan of anguish punctuated the violent smashing of glass, and he swung back to her, hands outstretched in a sick, impassioned plea. 'Why...why...why did you have to do this? Why, Gina?'

He groped the air in a blind attempt to pluck some understanding from it. 'To become...it was so unnecessary. I would have given you anything you wanted...anything!'

CHAPTER FIVE

ONE tiny part of Gina's mind, that part which clung obsessively to the paramount need to get the money for Debbie, that part actually gleaned hope from Liam's terrible words. But she couldn't tell him now, couldn't ask; he was destroying too much of her. She was crumbling... control slipping away. Her good reputation... everything soiled... even though what he said was so untrue, the very opposite of reality.

Her voice shook and her lips quivered as she tried to push out words. 'How can you think such a thing of me?'

His pain twisted into anger with her ineffectual attempt at denial. 'Still running from the truth, Gina?' he taunted, then lashed at her in contempt. 'I'd respect you more if you were at least honest about what you are!'

It was too much. He had struck too far. A blaze of fury cauterised the pain of his unwarranted accusations. The frustrations, the anguish, the frightening battle against time that was her day-to-day life; he knew nothing about it and hadn't cared enough to ask! His cruel assumptions about her hacked through the floodgates, and a bitter rage consumed her.

Wronged beyond endurance and wounded to the depths of her being, Gina flung herself at him, attacking with sheer animal mindlessness, fists flying wherever they could strike him, wanting to hurt as much as his vicious tongue had hurt her.

Liam made no attempt to defend himself. His face whitened with the force of her blows, then burnt a dull, painful red. She pummelled his chest and he took it with barely a flinch. She wanted to kill him but, in the end, the sheer stoicism with which he withstood the brunt of her mad fury defeated her.

Her arms hung limply at her sides, her fists smarting, her chest heaving in pained distress, tears of frustration streaming down her cheeks. 'I hate you for doing this to me, Liam Shannon. I hate you for thinking it. I hate you, hate you, hate you!'

'That's not true, Gina,' he said with a weariness of soul that echoed a terrible hollowness. His handsome face was ravaged, his eyes dark pools of anguish. 'And that's the hell of it. For both of us.'

She shook her head in helpless denial of anything he might say. 'I'm not what you think I am. I couldn't do such a thing. Nor even contemplate it. Never would I be a call-girl. Or...'

'Don't!' The cry tore from his throat and the next instant his arms were around her in a crushing embrace. 'We won't talk of it. We'll pretend...anything you like.' His hand roughly stroked her hair, pressing her head on to his shoulder as his voice rushed into an impassioned plea. 'Let me love you as I've dreamed of loving you, Gina. I'll wipe Vincente and all the rest out of your mind. I'll...'

'No...no...' A terrible pain constricted her chest. How could she show him the truth? Make him believe it?

'I promise you...' He dragged in a tortured breath. 'I don't care! I don't care what you've done, what you are...anything! I've wanted you...loved you... for so long; I can't let you go, not without at least showing you how it should have been. Not like the others you've had, Gina. You and me...'

His hand ran down her spine, pressing her into the hard male warmth of him, arousing her weakened body to an unwilling response. 'Stop it! Oh, please, stop it...' she sobbed, trying to push him away. 'You don't love me, Liam. If you did, you'd know I couldn't be...like that. You'd know...'

'The only thing I know is that you're in my arms, where you belong. Where you've always belonged,' he said with feverish possessiveness. 'Love me, Gina. Love me as you've always wanted to. Love me as I love you.' And he covered her wet face with hot, urgent kisses.

She felt her heart was breaking in two. 'Liam...Liam, don't you see...?'

'I see only you. Only you. As I've seen you every night for years. Just give me this night, Gina. I'll give you whatever you want...anything...'

'No! Oh, God! You can't do this to me!' she moaned, beside herself with distress.

'You can't deny me, Gina. Not when I know what I know now...'

'No! No!' she screamed, clawing blindly to be free of this unbearable torment.

Liam carried her with him, and all her kicking and flailing of arms and legs wrung nothing from him. It was as if he was anaesthetised to all pain except that which drove him relentlessly on. He fell on the bed with her, silencing all possible verbal protest with an onslaught of bruising kisses. She tore at his hair. She pounded his back. 'No! No! No!' she cried when she tore her mouth free.

'I'll give you everything,' he breathed harshly, and caught her hands, forcing them out to her sides. His body moved purposefully over hers, pinning her down, moving her legs apart, making her tremblingly aware of the hard core of his desire.

'You want me, Gina! You've never wanted any other man as you want me. I need to know that,' he said in a hoarse rasp that was more a despairing plea than a demand.

'Please, Liam...don't do this,' she begged, feeling her defences shattering against the need pulsing so strongly from him to her.

'Gina...' It was a tortured groan, and he rested his forehead on hers as he dragged in breath, his chest heaving over her flattened breasts. 'I have to feel you next to me. I have to hold you. I have to be inside you. I want to die there, Gina.'

The sheer extremity of his passion terrified her. He was beyond reason, yet she knew she would die if she gave in to him under these circumstances. 'It can't work, Liam. It won't be right,' she argued frantically. 'It can't be what you want.'

His eyes glittered down at her, not seeing the fear or the anguished plea for a stay of judgement. 'You're mine, Gina. I'll make you mine. For always and for ever!'

And he let her hands go, to wrap his arms around her, and roll her over and over the bed in a wild thrashing of wanting. And he kissed her. He kissed her with a savagery and a completeness that wiped everything from her mind but the dark passion she was succumbing to and the uncontrollable response his mouth evoked from hers.

For the first time in her life she lost herself to someone stronger than herself. He tore the whole fabric of her ordered existence apart, and she clung to him in fear, madness, excitement, surrender, to arms that bound her too relentlessly for her to fight, to lips that ravaged her soul, to a fate that was rushing too fast on her to evade.

'My darling...my love...my heart...my life...'

Liam breathed the words, burning her skin with them as he stripped off her clothes and trailed feverish kisses over her trembling nakedness. Tattered threads of sanity urged her to stop him, to at least make some attempt to fight for another chance, yet a treacherous sense of inevitability frayed those threads into meaningless wisps.

Too late...too late...her heart hammered the refrain with a finality that kept her still, even when Liam left her to tear off his own clothes. Like an angel of darkness he towered over her, emanating all the violent forces of hell-bent destruction, and nothing could contain them now. He had forced her down a path from which there was no retreat, no retracing the steps another way, no remoulding thoughts or opinions...just two worlds hurtling towards collision without any hope of a future.

And, insane as it was, Gina wanted to take him inside her and appease the demons that drove him, to give him the peace he craved, to die with him...because there could be no aftermath, no continuance...only this one fatal act of intimacy that would have to burn for eternity in her memory...Liam!

He came to her with an ugency that sent a convulsive thrill of desire through her entire body, but she thought...if it is only to be this once, then it must be all I could ever have...and she denied him a quick possession, shamelessly offering a slower satiation of the need to own.

Never had she felt anything like it: this wanton compulsion to tease, to taste, to provoke, to exicte, to savour every physical nuance of feeling and reaction; to immerse herself totally in touch and sensation. All previous inhibitions were utterly crushed as they drove each other to erotic extremes, fueling a sensual greed that grew ever more demanding until the ultimate giving and taking of self was a nerve-screeching need.

There was nothing...nothing in the whole world that could ever match the intense gratification of Liam's first surge inside her, the full, heavy thrust of him filling the want, the need, the emptiness that had craved for this final ecstatic union. Her body arched in exquisite pleasure, trembled on a pinnacle of exultation, then melted around him, fusing with him again and again as he stroked his possession with a wild, rhythmic mastery.

He took her through dimensions of feeling that Gina had never experienced before, would have thought impossible until now...and when he rolled her over so that she was straddled across his thighs, Gina revelled in the dominance he allowed her. But her momentary sense of control was explosively undermined when he thrust deep inside her, making her cry out with the quivering intensity of her pleasure.

'Liam...I can't!' she gasped incoherently.

'Gina...' It was a moan of longing, almost answered, and he rolled her back, dragging her legs around his hips as he plunged once more to the heart of her. 'Say yes to me...say yes, I want you...say yes, I love you...say yes, there's only me...only me...'

'Yes, yes, yes,' she cried.

Her arms lifted to hug him tightly as he sagged on top of her, depleted yet replete in the union of love.

'Gina...' he breathed with a fulfilled contentment that moved her to tears. She had been so wrong about Liam—so terribly, wretchedly wrong. She fiercely wished that she could roll the years back, that she had seen, known what it could have been like with him if only...

She closed her eyes, hating herself for the blind loyalty she had given to Jim. She had never belonged to her husband, not in this deep, riveting sense that involved her whole being. Liam had been right all along. He was her man...her mate. And yes, she wanted him. And yes, there was a bond, beyond knowledge or reason or any common sense at all. What else could it be but love? Only he...only he...

His arms encircled her, carrying her with him as he moved his weight aside. Enveloped in his warmth and strength, Gina allowed herself the tempting luxury of dreaming that nothing could ever separate them. If they didn't speak, if they just held on to each other, if time could stop now...

He stroked her back, her hair...so gently, caringly, lovingly...blissful. For a long time she lay with her head over his heart, denying all other existence but this. She was his. He was hers. And maybe this wasn't only an end, but a beginning to a future they could share, if only they could hang on to the togetherness.

But the silence grew heavy with torturous tentacles of thought that slithered around the guard she tried to keep against them. Gina could no longer be content merely to lie next to him. If he would not speak, she had to tell him how terribly mistaken he had been about her. And what was necessary for Debbie.

'Liam...' She started to raise her head, but his hand swiftly covered her movement, pressing stillness.

'Stay!' he whispered.

She sighed in tremulous compliance, quelling her desperate impatience to know his mind as well as his body. Liam twirled the long, silky strands of her hair around his fingers, weaving bonds that tied her to him.

'We'll make a world of our own where nothing else can ever touch us,' he said huskily.

Reality kept gnawing at her. If Liam was talking about any time beyond tonight, and she hoped quite desperately that he was, then he had to be told about Debbie. He had to accept her. Gina could never contemplate a world without her daughter. She drew on her courage, took a deep breath, and braved his displeasure.

'Liam, I can't...'

'Don't say that!'

The cutting ferocity of his command stabbed straight to her heart. Didn't he want to reach an understanding with her? Was physical intimacy all he needed?

With an abruptness that broke into her private agonising, he heaved her on to her back and leaned over her, his eyes ablaze with intense purpose.

'Listen to me, Gina. I don't care what you've done or why you did it. I'm in no position to blame you for anything. And I don't care. We'll put it all behind us. Leave the country. Live anywhere you want...'

A sickening wave of revulsion hit her stomach. He still believed that... Her mind clamped down on the hideous thought and fought it. And, despite what Liam believed, he still loved her. He wanted her to share his life anyway. Didn't such bigness of heart more than balance the wrong? But there was so much he had to know...

Her eyes searched his, hoping his heart was big enough to accept Debbie, too. 'I have a daughter, Liam.'

His face stiffened. 'Jim's child?'

'Of course she's Jim's child!' That he should even ask the question scraped over the deep hurt that still throbbed through her heart. Yet, if Liam would help her, any sacrifice was worth that end.

His taut face slowly relaxed into softness. 'I'll adopt her.'

'It's not that easy,' Gina sighed. 'I wish it were.'

She could ask for nothing more from his initial reaction, but Gina was all too aware of the problems inherent in the situation. What she was about to say was vitally important to any future happiness they might have together, and she watched Liam carefully, all her senses alert for negative signals.

'Debbie will have to accept you first, Liam. She's not a baby. She's four years old, and more sensitive than most children to how people feel about her,' Gina warned.

'So...I'll work it out,' he said with unwavering determination.

Gina prayed that he would not balk at the last hurdle. Accepting one small child and getting her to like him was one thing, sharing the responsibility of a child who might be handicapped all her life was quite another.

'That's not all, Liam. She's almost blind.'

The muscles around his mouth tightened. A line furrowed down between his eyebrows. Gina wasn't sure if the fractional change of expression was sympathetic concern or something else, but she had to spill out the whole truth now. If Liam really loved her as he said, he couldn't help but respond to all the anguish in her heart.

'If she doesn't have an operation soon, Liam, she'll be blind for life. There's a clinic in Los Angeles that has had some success in removing these cystic growths, but hers are so far back, near the brain...it's very highly specialised work. The doctors at Camperdown Children's Hospital say it's Debbie's only chance.'

Gina took a deep breath and plunged on to the critical question. 'I've done everything I can to get the money to pay for it. There's no public fund for cases like Debbie's. I don't own anything to raise a loan on. But I've got to get fifty thousand dollars so Debbie can have the operation. That money isn't easy to come by, and that's why... Liam, you must see... I must ask you...'

'Yes, I see,' he said in an oddly flat voice.

His face sagged into heavy, grim lines, and Gina sensed an indefinable withdrawal from her. It panicked her into a more anxious pleading for Debbie's cause.

'She's my daughter, Liam. I have to do everything that will help get her sight restored. She's so beautiful and loving, and I can't bear for her to be so terribly handicapped. I've been working around the clock on three different jobs, living on nothing . . . almost nothing . . .'

Why were his eyes so hard? Why had he gone so tense? She couldn't understand what seemed to be a stony lack of sympathy. 'So, whatever we share, Liam, I must put Debbie first,' she went on, driven by an ever-mounting need for his support. 'It can't be any other way. This is so critical to her whole life.'

'Of course,' he said, but his voice had a hollow ring to it. 'What a terrible time you've had . . . what agony of mind . . .' He settled back on the pillows, separating himself from her. 'Don't worry any more. I'll do everything you need.' The words seemed to trip out effortlessly, but his fist was tightly clenched, the knuckles showing white.

The panicky feeling settled into a tight ache of fear in Gina's chest. Was he jealous of her love for her own child? Jim's child? Perhaps Liam could never forgive her for choosing Jim, and with Debbie a living reminder of that marriage . . .

The memory of the pain Liam had revealed to her this afternoon smote her heart. Gina silently vowed she would do everything possible to make it up to him, to erase that grievous beginning with the love she would give him throughout the years to come.

Perhaps she had stressed Debbie's plight too much. It had been the only thing on her mind for so long. But to Liam, both Debbie's existence and her blindness had probably been intrusive shocks at a time when he had wanted nothing to intrude on the love that was theirs alone. She should have waited a bit longer, should have made him feel more wanted in her life.

Desperate to re-establish communication, Gina ran caressing fingertips over the warm, sensitive skin from under his arm down to his waist. The convulsive shudder that followed the light touch gave her a thrill of power, and she smiled as he caught her hand and held it tight.

'I didn't mean that there wouldn't be any time for us, Liam,' she said softly. 'We could be together. If that's what you want.'

His fingers almost crushed hers, tightening until they hurt. He swung his legs off the bed and stood, releasing her hand as if the touch of her was suddenly anathema to him. The muscles of his back became rigidly taut as he straightened. He turned to her, his face stamped with a dark, stony pride, his eyes empty of all emotion. Whatever he was thinking was completely hidden from her.

'So the race has been run and you got what you needed,' he said tonelessly. 'Underneath it all...the veneer...most people are the same. You must forgive me for being cynical.'

Her blood ran cold. She stared at him in pained bewilderment as he rounded the bed and picked up his jacket from the floor.

He flicked her a thin little smile. 'Don't worry, my dear. The money is no problem. I said I'd give you anything you wanted, and I will. You certainly gave me what I wanted, even down to the words I wanted to hear. A great performance.' The smile twisted with self-contempt. 'Stupid of me. I've always had this blind spot where you are concerned, Gina. I'd do anything for you.'

'Liam ... no! You mustn't think like that!' she gasped, scrambling to get off the bed to deny whatever feelings were twisting him into a rejection of what they had just shared. Her hands lifted in beseeching appeal. 'It wasn't a performance! I don't do that sort of thing! Not with any man. Not even Jim. And what I had with him doesn't compare with what we had together, Liam. You've got to believe me! No other man could have given me what we just shared.'

He withdrew a cheque-book from the inside pocket of his jacket, and walked over to the writing-table, moving like an automaton that was immune to her agonised plea.

'Liam, for God's sake! Listen to me!' Gina begged. 'You've got the whole situation wrong! Entirely and terribly wrong! Tell me what I did. Tell me what I said to make you change like this. I swear to you, you've misunderstood!'

He didn't look up, nor did he stop writing. 'I have my needs too, Gina. Here's your money for services rendered. You can clear the cheque at the bank tomorrow morning.' The words were spoken in a cold, flat monotone. 'You'll have no trouble with it, I assure you. I wouldn't let Jim's daughter go blind. He was my best friend ... in better times.'

Jim! Liam was underlining his total rejection of her. Gina's voice shook with the force of her need to know why he was doing this. Was he exacting the most terrible revenge on her for what he thought she had done to him?

'I won't take your money, Liam. Not for that reason. I've never given myself to a man for money. Not ever. And never will. You can check out the Australian Interpreters' Company. It's a legitimate service for foreign businessmen needing help, not a...a call-girl racket. Ask Mr Vincente...'

His eyes flared briefly at her as he straightened up, then narrowed into hard slits. 'I'll find my salvation, Gina. Somehow. Some way.'

He breathed deeply, and there was a slight tremble of his lower lip as he quietly added, 'You did what you had to do. And I did what I had to do. But we're too different. Have different ways. There is no future. There was never really any beginning. But let us finish it...with some dignity.'

A painful flush burnt over her nakedness, and Gina wrung her hands in helpless despair. 'Liam. I...I love you. I didn't know it before, but I...'

He stiffened as though she had slapped him. 'Please, don't go on. There's no need for more acting. You gave...more than value for money. It was the catharsis I needed to work out my life. I thank you for giving me your beautiful body. I hope you found some pleasure in mine. But let us be honest, Gina. There is no need for more words.' He held out the cheque to her.

Gina backed away, shaking her head, tears spurting into her eyes, trickling down her cheeks, the pain in her chest so bad that she had to hug her arms across it. 'Don't do this to us, Liam,' she begged. 'Not now...not when we've just come together...'

He took a step towards her, and the stiff mask of dignity suddenly cracked with violent emotion. His eyes were searing stabs of agonised frustration. His face contorted with raging conflict. He jerked away from her and slammed the cheque down on the desk.

'For your own sake—and mine—get dressed! You have what you want! Go! Go, before you destroy me completely!'

He turned on his heel and strode furiously away, his explosive commands ringing in her ears and slowly, slowly thumping into her heart—death-blows to any possibility of a relationship between them.

Gina sank down on the bed, trembling with shock, and too dazed and bereft to cope with any-thing. She had tried to make him under-stand...what else could she have done?

She heard the tinkle of a bottle and glass; a couple of doors being opened and shut; the jangle of clothes-hangers. She vaguely remembered cupboards lining the wall near the bar, and realised that Liam was dressing. The slam of another door punctuated his departure.

It was over. Liam had said it; yet it had never really started. And how could it, with such hope-lessly misconceived foundations? Everything at cross purposes. Misjudgements. She and Liam had been ill-fated from the start.

Finish it with some dignity. But dignity was a terribly empty feeling, and Gina couldn't dredge up enough inner fortitude to sustain it. She had found love and lost it in the space of one short night, and she simply couldn't cope with the devastated battleground of so many tumultuous emotions.

Her gaze fell on one of her red sandals, tossed against the wall. Get dressed and go, her mind echoed. She pushed herself off the bed and listlessly picked up her clothes, one by one. It was harder to put them on. Her hands fumbled. She felt drained of all strength, unsteady on her feet.

Then there was the cheque. For Debbie. Gina sank on to the chair at the writing-desk. She stared down at the slip of paper that could make her daughter see again. Fifty thousand dollars. Liam's signature danced before her eyes, taunting her with the totally unjust judgements he had made.

Gina knew beyond any shadow of a doubt that, if she took the cheque, she would stand forever condemned in Liam's mind. It would be confirmation that she had given herself to him for money...for Debbie's sake. And not for the feelings he aroused in her.

If she didn't take it, would he come after her? Would he realise he had been totally wrong and beg her forgiveness? Even if he did, could she ever forget his pitiless lack of faith? She felt almost numb right now, but the hurt was a dull throb, waiting to burst the containment of shock and tear her apart.

Love and hatred were so closely aligned that it was difficult to separate one from the other, and she and Liam had made it too easy to hate one another. She hadn't trusted him, and now he didn't trust her. They might have crossed those mistrustful barriers tonight, but it was too late. Always too late for them. Always the wrong time or the wrong place or the wrong people around them.

A wrenching grief for all the might-have-beens blurred her eyes with more tears. She picked up the cheque. It represented the only possible good that could come out of this miserable affair. Liam could afford the money. Debbie needed it. And one life would be brighter for it.

Gina folded the cheque and tucked it in her handbag, hating the necessity that drove her to do it. She picked up the pen that Liam had dropped, a mind-savaging sense of loss prompting her to write some message...some acknowledgement that Liam might understand. The pristine blotter in the leather writing-block tempted her beyond caring whether it was right or wrong. Her hand moved, writing slowly, laboriously.

'I wish it could have been different——'

She didn't sign her name. Pointless! The words were probably pointless. It didn't really matter. Nothing mattered any more. Except Debbie. She dropped the pen, pushed herself to her feet and forced herself to walk away, out of Liam's suite, out of the hotel, away from what might have been...if it could have been different.

CHAPTER SIX

THE TELLER slid the bankbook back under the grille, the new entry all typed up, delivered with an inquisitive smile. Gina whispered a nervous 'thank you' and moved aside to give way to the next person on the queue. Her hand shook as she opened the book to check the amount that had been accredited to her. The figures were there . . . stamped, ratified, absolute proof that she had the money.

She walked out of the bank in a numb daze. There was no joy in having the money, no triumph, no sense of achievement. Her mind insisted that only the end result mattered. If Debbie's operation was a success, then the cost to herself and Liam would be justified. If it wasn't a success . . . But she couldn't let herself consider that possibility. Debbie was going to see again. She had to. Otherwise, the price would have been too great.

Gina forced her feet to move more quickly. There was so much to do—arrangements to make—and they had to be done as soon as possible. No time to waste. She couldn't afford to think of Liam, couldn't let the hurt keep clouding her mind the way it had done all morning. It would sap her will to go on and do what had to be done. All her energy had to be concentrated on getting Debbie to Los Angeles.

Afterwards ... But she couldn't think about afterwards, either. The longer she put off thinking about Liam, the better. The day might come when the memory of last night and the pain of loss would become bearable, but not yet, not in the foreseeable future. To function at all, she had to keep the pain contained.

When she returned home, Gina found Esme in a fever of inspiration. Her artistic triumph of yesterday was definitely going to be surpassed today, and she had appointed Debbie as chief adviser on the new composition. The conversation between them was so animated and wildly imaginative that Gina was almost bemused out of her preoccupation with Liam's cheque. She hadn't told Esme about it until now, out of fear that Liam might have cancelled it, but there was no putting off the moment any longer.

'I've got the money for the operation, Esme,' she announced quietly.

A vivid splash of purple streaked across the canvas as Esme turned from her easel, paintbrush still poised in her hand, her mouth wide open in astonishment. She shook her head. 'Did I hear right?'

'Yes. I have to go and see Dr Halston. He said he would organise the Los Angeles end, get a fixed date for us and ...'

'But how, Gina?' Esme broke in, stunned bewilderment swiftly changing to sharp concern. 'Have you gone and robbed the bank?'

A pained little smile twisted Gina's lips. 'Don't worry, Esme. No one's going to come running to take it back. The money... was given... to me.'

Esme's mobile face was suddenly very still. Her merry brown eyes lost their twinkle as they studied Gina's expression: the tightness around her mouth, the shadows under her eyes, the bleakness that stared back at her, grim with purpose but empty of all feeling.

'What did you do, Gina?' she asked softly. 'If you'd known anyone with that kind of money, you would have approached them long ago.'

Gina held rigidly to her hard-won control. 'Don't ask me, Esme,' she said flatly. 'I don't want to talk about it. Ever. Just accept that we've got it.'

'Gina...'

Concern, understanding, compassion—all throbbed into the soft pronouncement of her name. The silence stretched for several agonised moments. Then the big woman with the big heart pushed a warmly encouraging smile across her face.

'Those doctors in Los Angeles had better be ready, willing and able,' she said with cheerful belligerence. 'Get them lined up. Debbie and I will plan a celebration dinner. Today is a great day!'

'Yes. A great day,' Gina echoed, gratefully falling in with Esme's game.

And not once in the days that followed did her friend ever let her down. Only Esme's joyous optimism kept Gina going. It bubbled from her in a buoyant stream that lifted Gina out of the darker thoughts that haunted her nights. Debbie was imbued with excited anticipation at the wondrous thought of seeing all that Esme had painted for her in her mind, and just to see her little face aglow with happiness eased the constant ache in Gina's heart.

The operation was scheduled, their flight to the United States booked. Gina was shocked to discover that the lowering of the exchange rate of the Australian dollar during the last year meant she still wasn't over-burdened with money. She needed every cent of her savings to cover the shortfall. In fact, she had barely enough to cover her living expenses while she stayed in Los Angeles. But she would manage. Somehow. As she always did.

Esme accompanied them to Mascot Airport and saw them off. Debbie consumed most of Gina's attention on the long flight, with the need to have everything that was going on around her explained in detail. Once they had arrived at their destination, Gina ran herself ragged on nervous energy—booking Debbie into the clinic, talking to the medical staff, finding cheap lodgings, working out how best to eke out her meagre resources. When she fell into bed, she slept the sleep of utter exhaustion.

The days that followed were like a nightmare. It wasn't until after Debbie's operation was completed that Gina could relax enough to allow thoughts of Liam to filter into her mind. She sat at her daughter's bedside, stroking her soft little hand, waiting for her to regain consciousness so that she could soothe any fear or pain. Debbie's head was swathed in bandages, but the surgeon assured Gina that, when the bandages came off, her daughter's vision would be completely unimpaired. And Liam had made that possible.

However deeply he despised her, and however wrongly so, he had given her what he thought she wanted. The least she could do was write and thank him, on Debbie's behalf. But the more Gina thought about a letter to Liam, the more tempted she was to write other things, to spill out the yearning in her heart, to try again to explain, to reach past the terrible misunderstandings that had torn them apart.

But the remembrance of that last look he had given her filled Gina with despair. Whatever she wrote to Liam would only stir the utmost contempt. Let us finish it with some dignity, he had said, yet...everything within her writhed against following that edict.

She heaved a deep sigh. Liam had got along without her for six years. Surely she could do the same. It wasn't as if she was alone, as Liam had been. She had Debbie and Esme. Liam had no one at all. No one... Gina shivered as she remembered how he had spent those six years.

Her daughter stirred, the limp fingers curling convulsively around Gina's. 'Mummy?'

'Yes,' Gina whispered, a lump of emotion filling her throat. 'Everything's all right, Debbie. Soon, in a few days, you'll be able to see again. And your eyes will keep getting better. In a couple of weeks you'll be able to see everything.'

The sweet, childish mouth quivered into a smile. 'Just like Esme said? I'll be able to see her paintings?'

'Yes, my love. You'll be able to see all her paintings,' Gina assured her huskily.

Gina wrote a long letter to Esme that night, telling her about the operation and pouring out all the love and gratitude she felt towards the woman who had done so much for Debbie and herself. Then, on the same wave of sweeping emotion, and despite what Liam might think about it, she wrote to him, making no mention of what had happened between them, but thanking him deeply for what he had made possible for her daughter.

She did not expect a reply from Liam, nor did she get one. Nevertheless, the joy of sharing Debbie's experience of sight did much to balance the pain of losing Liam. The days after the bandages were removed were both scary and exciting. First there was the slow and careful exposure to the glare of light; then the glow of recognition in her daughter's eyes; the wonderful morning when Gina took Debbie for a walk outside in the grounds of the clinic... It was all so intensely rewarding that Gina assured herself that this had been worth any sacrifice.

Debbie was due to receive her final discharge, and Gina was already preparing for their return to Sydney when an extraordinary letter arrived from Esme. Inside the folded pages was a cheque for two thousand dollars! Hardly believing what she saw,

Gina swiftly turned to the thick sheaf of writing for an explanation.

'I have sold a painting!!!'

Laughter bubbled up in Gina's throat. In her mind's eye she could see Esme dancing around in blissful triumph, declaring her genius to one and all. Gina read on, immensely pleased that someone had at last recognised her friend's great talent.

> 'You are to spend this money on taking Debbie to Disneyland. Show her all that there is to see and wonder at and enjoy. Celebrate! Be happy! Nothing could give me more pleasure than giving this pleasure to the two people I hold most dear in my heart.'

Tears rushed into Gina's eyes. For several minutes she wept unashamedly, intensely moved by the unflagging generosity of Esme's bountiful soul. Disneyland—it was just what Esme would think of, and she was so right, so wonderfully right. For Debbie, it would be the most magical experience she could possibly have: a feast of colourful sights and fantasies to celebrate the end of darkness. Esme had the purest and most blessed genius of all...that which embodied the art of giving.

Gina mopped up her tears and picked up the letter again. Her heart began thumping erratically as she raced through the pages, devouring and dissecting every word that Esme wrote.

> 'I am on cloud nine! Remember you took out an Italian gentleman called Bruno Vincente? He is adorable. Not only has he

got beautiful manners, but he has the perception to appreciate my art and is madly eager for me to paint more in my new style. He says I am a Primitive! A Magnificent Primitive! That is the way he talks. And the way his eyes flash with excitement at me! I keep wanting to hug him, but I don't want to frighten him off. Not yet. He is rather little. But what a marvellous, big mind he has!

You'll never guess how I came to meet him. Remember the man who returned your handbag? His name is Liam Shannon, and he knew you years ago, before you married Jim. He turned up again and introduced himself, and of course I invited him in and told him all about you and Debbie—how Jim died at the wrong time and how desperate you were about Debbie, and how you were working around the clock for her sake. He was most concerned, but I assured him everything was all right...now. At last. Wonderfully all right!

'He saw my garden painting hanging on the wall and asked if it was for sale. He offered me five thousand dollars for it, right then and there. Sold, I said! He took my painting with him and showed it to Bruno, who has been on my doorstep ever since. The darling man. Bruno says I need an agent. He says not to sell another thing until I have enough paintings for a showing at a gallery.

He is going to organise it all and make me famous. And rich!!!

'So, my dears, have the loveliest time at Disneyland, and don't come home with a cent of that money left unspent. I'm going to paint like a demon, and we'll never have to worry about money again. Bruno's opinion is thought of highly in the art world, so he knows what he is talking about. Isn't that marvellous? Of course, I always knew I had genius. Until Bruno, though, no one else could see it. He has an absolutely brilliant mind!

'I told Liam Shannon you would be home in a few weeks. He is terribly tense. Someone ought to teach him how to relax. It's all very well to have an eye for a good painting, but it's plain to see he doesn't know how to enjoy life.

'Tell Debbie I owe all my success to her, and I'll have lots of pictures painted for her to see, and give her lots of hugs and kisses from me.

All my love,
Esme.

Gina read the parts about Liam over and over again, interpreting his behaviour in so many different ways that her head ached from the sheer frenzy of her agonising thoughts.

Why had he gone to Esme? Did he have an eye for a good painting, or did he have another motive entirely in offering Esme so much money for it?

He had said he would do anything for her. Was this an indirect way of ensuring that she was in no need? How much had Esme told him? When he had spoken to Mr Vincente, had he asked about her and found out the truth? Why hadn't he got in touch with her, answered her letter?

The questions were endless, and there were no certain answers to any of them. But gradually hope was born of Esme's letter... a fragile hope that Gina nursed continually. Surely there was no reason for Liam to visit Esme, unless it wasn't finished for him. For all that he might have wanted to let it go, he hadn't been able crush what he felt for her. Not completely. So there had to be hope.

Gina wanted to go home immediately, but she couldn't deprive Debbie of Disneyland. True to the spirit which Esme had insisted upon, Gina booked a room at The Holiday Inn, Anaheim, only two blocks from the park and providing a convenient shuttle service. They spent five happy days there.

Every morning they went off to Disneyland, but, despite the fabulous attractions of the park, both Gina and Debbie were tired out by lunch time, and they returned to the inn to sleep through the afternoons. Gina felt an almost constant lethargy, and supposed it was caused by the cumulative strain of having worked so hard for so long. Now that she had time on her hands, she didn't know how to cope with it. Nevertheless, it was a relief to think she would only have to handle one job in future.

Debbie thoroughly enjoyed the flight home, and being met at the airport by Esme was the ultimate bliss. Esme was resplendent in a billowing caftan that was printed with brilliant parrots and exotic flowers. Beaded and feathered combs were stuck haphazardly in her orange hair. She literally enveloped Debbie in gorgeous Technicolor and the warmest of love as she hugged her and cradled her in her arms. It was a beautiful homecoming... except Liam wasn't there.

Gina's eyes darted around the airport terminal, hoping to see him waiting somewhere in the background. Her intense disappointment was totally unreasonable, she told herself. If Liam wanted to see her again, a busy airport was unlikely to be his choice of venue.

She wondered if she could go and visit him, thank him personally... and decided she could not. Liam knew where she lived. There was nothing to stop him from visiting her any time he liked, *if* he liked. He knew Esme would not turn him away. And surely her letter could only have been read as encouraging, if he wanted to be encouraged.

Esme and Debbie chattered like birds all the way home in the taxi. Gina idly noticed the newspaper bill-boards in the streets—huge headlines proclaiming a new discovery of oil. She had been away for over a month, and had seen no Australian news in that time. She wondered where the oil was. Certainly the national economy needed a lift. Maybe the Australian dollar would go up. Not that it mattered now. It was too late to help her with the exchange rate.

Gina was too tired to do anything but go to bed when they arrived home. She was sick the next morning. Esme fussed over her, insisting that she stay in bed all day. Jet lag, Gina thought. Her system was out of order. A long sleep would set her right again. But the same nausea hit her the next morning. And the next.

'You're totally run-down, Gina,' Esme declared. 'Skin and bone. I'm going to get you on a proper diet. Feed you up. And you're not to think of looking for a job until I say so.'

Gina couldn't find the energy to argue. She didn't seem to have any energy at all. It was much easier to let Esme mother her. She must have picked up some bug from all the crowds at Disneyland. It was lucky that Debbie had not succumbed as well. Gina kept telling herself she would feel better soon. Then she would get her life in order. Was Liam ever going to come back into it again?

Bruno Vincente called by daily to see Esme, who painted furiously, much to his and Debbie's delight. It was obvious that he adored Esme's company as much as she adored his. He did not mention Liam Shannon. Gina didn't ask about him. The memory of Liam's ruthlessness with Bruno that fateful night at the Regent was an embarrassment to them all.

It was not until Gina became conscious of a prickling tenderness in her breasts that a frightening suspicion dawned on her. Her mind almost froze with the shock of the idea as she forced herself to count back the weeks. There were too many of them. Far too many.

With the hectic upheavals in her life, the strain of getting things done and all the travelling, she hadn't even noticed that one other regularity had slipped by her. Perhaps her emotional stress had upset her hormones, Gina frantically argued, but how to discount the lethargy and the nausea and the tingling in her breasts? It all fitted together... And what, in God's name, was she going to do if she *was* pregnant?

She hadn't even thought of it that night with Liam. He hadn't given her time to think of it, she thought bitterly. He had virtually forced himself on her, and now it seemed he didn't want to have anything to do with her. He probably wouldn't even believe that the child was his! And what a savage irony that was!

The blackest of black despairs descended on Gina. How on earth was she going to cope with a baby? She wouldn't be able to work. She would have to apply for government assistance...or live on Esme's charity. And that was so unfair after all Esme had done for them already. It was all so terribly unfair! She had just got Debbie right again and had been looking forward to leading a relatively normal life...and Liam...Liam...where was he? Why didn't he come? Was it only concern for Jim's daughter that had brought him to Esme that day?

Esme found her in the bathroom in floods of tears, and led her back to bed, clucking like a mother hen. 'This won't do, Gina. This won't do at all. You're heading for a nervous breakdown. I'm going to ring my doctor and make an appointment for this afternoon. You need help to get over this, whatever it is. Something's wrong. It's gone on for too long.'

And it would go on a lot longer... all her life, Gina thought hysterically, but she tried to calm down, for Esme's sake. And it was best she saw a doctor. Maybe she was wrong. It could be anaemia, or some wretched virus or...

But all such feeble hopes were shattered once the doctor had examined her. 'Pregnant,' he said with a benevolent smile. 'About seven weeks along, I should think.'

'Yes,' Gina agreed faintly. She hadn't really expected any other answer, but the confirmation was like a lump of lead on her heart.

'You need some iron tablets...'

He went on and on, and Gina kept nodding like an automaton.

'And come back for a check-up next month. My nurse will make an appointment for you.'

'Thank you,' Gina managed stiffly.

She did all the right things: made the appointment, took the prescriptions to the pharmacy and got the tablets the doctor recommended, even stopped at a baby-shop and stared at the tiny garments displayed in the window. But she felt defeated. Jim's death... Debbie's blindness... she had had the will to cope with everything up until now, but somehow it had slipped away from her, that strong will that could drive her to manage against all the odds.

She walked home with the slow gait and the unseeing gaze of a zombie. It was as if the new life that was growing inside her had reduced her to a dead shell, a vehicle that had to keep going, yet was totally lost to any purpose of its own.

She hesitated at Esme's gate, reluctant to face her friend's enquiring concern, yet there was nowhere else to go, nothing else to be done but tell Esme the truth. Her shoulders drooped in weary resignation as she pushed open the gate, stepped up to the front porch, inserted her key in the door and opened it.

Debbie's high, excited voice floated out from the kitchen, extolling the wonders of Disneyland. Gina closed the door and walked down the hall. She reached the doorway to the kitchen and stopped dead, feeling as though she had been punched in the heart.

Liam! Liam with Debbie sitting on his knee, her little face lifted to his, glowing with pleasure at his rapt attention; Liam expensively dressed in a sober grey suit, his handsome face set in whimsical amusement, one arm encircling Debbie, the other hand holding open a children's picture-book.

Other books and soft toys and beautifully dressed dolls were piled high on the kitchen table. Discarded boxes and wrapping paper were strewn around the floor. Esme had abandoned her painting and seemed enthralled with a jigsaw puzzle. And in front of her easel was a Christmas tree, aglow with tinsel and brilliant baubles and coloured lights. Christmas in June for a child who had never seen the colour of Christmas!

Gina's heart burst into accelerated activity, but her mind was still too dazed to grasp what Liam meant by all this. Was it only compassion for a child . . . Jim's daughter? First the money for the operation, then buying Esme's painting to make Disneyland possible, now Christmas . . .

As if he had suddenly sensed her presence, Liam's gaze lifted and stabbed across the room at her. 'Mummy's home!' he said, and in an instant he had tossed the book on to the table and was on his feet, hoisting Debbie up against his shoulder and holding her firmly in his arms.

Debbie giggled, throwing him an adoring glance before beaming excitedly at Gina. 'Look at what Liam gave me, Mummy! And he said he would take me out on his boat and go to the zoo and . . . and what else, Liam?' she breathed, her arms curling eagerly around his neck.

Liam's eyes glittered triumphantly at Gina as he dropped a kiss on her daughter's forehead. 'Anything you want, sweetheart,' he promised. 'With me, the whole world can be your playground. Just say the word.'

'What word?' Debbie crowed.

'Hmmm . . . let me see now . . . what's the magic word?' he teased as he carried Debbie towards Gina.

'Tell me! Tell me!' Debbie pleaded, only too eager to say anything he suggested.

Liam's eyes bored into Gina's, darkly challenging, and she knew he felt no softness for her. For some ruthlessly diabolical purpose of his own, he was using her innocent daughter as a weapon against her.

He raised a quizzical eyebrow at Debbie. 'Do you love me?'

'Yes!' Debbie declared, almost strangling him with her fervour.

'Ah, yes...that's the magic word!' His gaze returned to Gina, diamond-hard. 'What other proof do you need, Gina?' he drawled, driving the words home with the subtlety of a sledge-hammer. 'Your daughter accepts me without any reservation whatever.'

Debbie's acceptance of him... Gina vividly recalled saying that it wasn't enough for Liam to adopt her. But there was far more to love than showering a child with gifts. It was so easy to impress with the wealth that Liam had at his disposal. Would he be so generous with his personal attention tomorrow, and the next day, and the next?

He smiled, for Debbie's benefit, not Gina's. 'Now we only need your mummy to say the magic word, and we can all be happy together,' he said with persuasive indulgence, winning a totally infatuated little girl to his side with the consummate ease of a master tactician.

'Say yes, Mummy! Say yes,' Debbie urged excitedly.

'Say yes to what, Liam?' Gina asked, wanting another chance with him, but wary of the threat-

ening relentlessness with which he was ma-
noeuvring her on to new ground.

The glitter in his eyes intensified, becoming
infinitely dangerous, and the tension emanating
from him held all the coiled menace of a trap about
to be sprung.

'Say yes, you love me, Gina. Say yes, you'll
marry me.'

CHAPTER SEVEN

LIAM still wanted her, but he wasn't offering love
this time. He simply intended to have her, regardless of the cost to her or to Debbie or to anyone
else. The cynical use of her daughter against her in
order to get his own way showed the total ruthlessness of the man. Gina bitterly berated herself
for her stupid dreams. Hadn't he already demon-
strated clearly and painfully that, to Liam Shannon,
only his needs counted?

Her eyes met his challenge with weary mockery.
'You don't love me, Liam. You never did and you
don't now. You only want me.'

His mouth took on a sardonic tilt. 'Let's say I'm
obsessional about it.'

'And totally blind to anything else,' she accused,
burning with the injustice of his judgements about
her.

'That's not true, Gina. I know what money can
buy.'

It was a deliberate taunt, and she flinched as
though he had struck her full in the face.

'Stop it!' The sharp command from Esme
whipped across the room. 'You two mustn't go on
at each other like this. I love you both and...'

'Don't interfere, Esme!' Liam replied with steely
dismissiveness, his eyes not even flickering an ac-

knowledgement of the interruption. 'These matters run too deep for you to possibly understand.'

Esme charged across the room, her formidable figure inflating with outrage. 'This is madness, what you're doing, and I won't stand for it!' she declared.

Liam's gaze did not release Gina's for a moment, holding her with a power that tied her to him beyond the realms of reason. 'Then leave us, Esme!' he warned, and his low voice carried a ferocity that should have driven anyone away.

But not Esme. She stood her ground and fearlessly protested, 'You're using Debbie as a pawn to get what you want, and I . . .'

'No! Gina did that!' Liam stated bitingly. He turned a forbidding face to Esme, making each word a telling force. 'Gina made it a condition—Debbie had to accept me if there was to be any future in our relationship. So here I am, Esme. With the child that can make or break us.'

His mouth curled into a wicked mockery of a smile that held no mercy. 'So we'll see if there's any future for us now. Gina might decide it's to her own and Debbie's advantage to give a lifelong performance.'

His eyes flicked back to Gina, cutting like lasers into her soul. 'We are all hanging on your answer, my dear.'

In a moment of mind-jolting revelation, Gina saw how deeply she had hurt him. First she had chosen Jim, and when Liam had thought she was finally his, revealing himself to the most vulnerable core of his being, then she had dealt him wounds that were even worse than he had dealt her. She at least had known herself innocent of selling herself; Liam had been led to believe that the love they had shared was a pretence on her part . . . to pay for Debbie's operation!

Yet here he was, still fighting for her, caught in the grip of an obsessional need that would not give him any peace until he had her.

He would never believe that she loved him now, no matter what she said or did. It was too late. Always too late with Liam. Yet, wounded as he was, he still did not want to live without her. And she didn't want to live without him. Gina did not stop to think of the consequences. Fearlessly, she raised her head to the man who had been driven to the edge of madness for love of her, and spoke straight from her heart.

'I love you, Liam. I know that now. And yes, I will marry you.'

His face tightened. 'I thought you might say that.' His words held a quiet venom, and his eyes glittered with bitter intensity. 'But I'm not going to die wondering if you mean those words or not. I intend to marry you, Gina. But there are a few conditions that you need to fulfil first.'

Her head whirled. Had she been wrong? Was he only here to slap the same kind of rejection in her face as she had given him? 'What conditions?' she asked, unable to stop herself from holding on to him as long as she could, no matter how deep the torment he was intent on inflicting.

He turned to Esme and handed Debbie across to her. 'Take Debbie up the street and buy her an ice-cream. I want to be alone with Gina.'

Esme tucked Debbie on to her hip with all the fierce protectiveness of a lioness with its cub. She drew herself up to her most majestic height, her eyes flaring a dire warning. 'You're a terrible man, Liam Shannon! I don't care what reasons you have. If you hurt Gina, I'll tear your black heart out myself.'

The ultimatum won no concession whatsoever from Liam, who might have been carved in stone for all the words meant to him. Esme threw an anxious look at Gina, who wearily nodded her agreement to Liam's demand. She marched off without another word, and Gina deeply regretted not having told her about Liam and what he had done for Debbie.

With the closing of the door after them, Gina felt more alone and vulnerable than she had ever felt in her life, but she faced up to Liam with a desperate kind of courage. Somehow she had to change his mind about her.

Unexpectedly, he stepped forward and slid an arm around her shoulders. Gina's legs almost sagged beneath her as he led her over to the kitchen table. She couldn't tell him about the baby now. He would read it as another calculating motive for accepting his proposal of marriage. Or even a plan to get him to marry her in the first place. He might even accuse her of trying to foist another man's child on to him.

'Sit down, Gina,' he commanded, holding out a chair for her.

Gina gratefully sank into it. Not only did her legs feel wobbly, her whole body was shaken by the conflict of emotions that Liam's presence evoked.

He didn't sit down himself. Gina watched apprehensively as he withdrew a long business envelope from his inner jacket pocket. From this he took a sheaf of papers, opened them out, reached into his pocket again for a pen, then placed them in front of her. He pointed to a pencilled cross at the end of one page. 'I want your signature here, Gina.'

She stared uncomprehendingly at the page for several moments before the name, NECSEC, loomed out at her. A burning rush of colour stained her cheeks as she darted a shame-faced look at him. 'I don't understand.'

'I'm transferring ownership of these shares that you recommended so highly. Without you, I'd never have bought them,' he reminded her pointedly. 'I want you to have them.'

'You know they're worthless,' she cried, tears of mortification welling into her eyes as she shoved the papers away. 'And you know I only recommended them to . . . to hit back at you. I'm sorry I did it. I . . .'

She shook her head in hopeless distress, too ashamed of the malice she had once felt to look at him. 'I thought you were out to hurt me, and I wanted to hurt you back. I realise now that I only hurt myself. I'm sorry. I hope you can get some of your money back on them.'

His harsh laugh drew her bewildered gaze. 'Don't you know that NECSEC shares are the hottest property on the market? One of their subsidiaries has discovered oil. This little parcel is now worth over half a million dollars.'

She stared at him in dazed disbelief.

'It's been in all the newspapers,' he told her, his eyes mocking her apparent ignorance.

Gina recalled the headlines she had seen on the way home from the airport, but she hadn't realised, or bothered, reading about something that didn't affect her.

Liam laughed without humour. 'Don't you know that every time you go against me, it always works to my advantage? I hate to think what would happen if you ever came my way! I'd probably be ruined overnight.'

'Thank God you weren't hurt by what I did to you,' Gina murmured, relieved of one guilt over her behaviour towards him.

'It never meant a tinker's curse to me!' he retorted savagely. 'I bought those shares for one reason only. To get some time with you. But now...' He stepped around to the end of the table and leaned his hands on it, his body bending forward, pushing his face closer to hers. The challenge in his eyes held a feverish recklessness. 'Now, Gina, now they're going to do so much more! One way or another they're going to decide the rest of your life!'

She stared wildly at him, trying to comprehend what he was saying and failing miserably. 'I don't understand what you want from me, Liam.'

'You almost convince me that you're not acting,' he mocked. 'But it's not that difficult to understand, Gina.' He pushed the papers back in front of her and straightened up, his face set in arrogant command. 'Sign the transfer. It's a very simple procedure. Pick up the pen and write your name.'

'But why are you doing this?' she persisted. It made no sense to her at all.

'I want you to be independently wealthy,' he answered with cold asperity.

'And I'll never see you again. Is that it, Liam?' she asked heavily.

'On the contrary. I'll come back in exactly sixty days. Counting from now. Then, and for the last time, I shall ask you to marry me. What answer you choose is entirely up to you. You'll have no...economic pressures...on you. No stress from me. You really should know your own mind—and heart—after two worry-free months.'

His mouth stretched into a sardonic smile. 'You can have the pleasure of telling me then to go to hell, if you like. It won't be any change for me, since that's where I habitually live anyway. Or you can accept me, and we'll spend our lives together, with the greatest happiness, I should think. But it's up to you.'

His whole face tightened into grimly determined lines. 'And the reason I do this is because I will not be tortured for the rest of my life by the thought that you only married me for the money I can give you and your daughter.'

'You think that's why... why I said... yes... to you just now.' Sadness welled up in her as she forced out the words. That he could think so badly of her, and be so generous...

'Money does strange things to people,' he mused bitterly, and there was hard accusation in his eyes. 'I've seen it often. Some people might even go to bed with a man for the money to prevent a child from going blind...'

'I didn't do that!' Gina denied vehemently, then grasped the chance to set the record straight. 'I've never gone to bed with anyone for money. You wouldn't listen to me, or believe me. But I never did. Not with you. Or anyone!'

He turned abruptly away from her with what Gina thought was a gesture of contempt.

It goaded her into counter-accusation. 'You know you forced me, Liam. I... I couldn't stop you. You know that,' she pleaded.

He strolled around to the opposite side of the table. Very deliberately, he picked up one of the dolls he had bought for Debbie, and re-arranged its arms so that they reached out to him. 'Everything I've ever got from you was forced, Gina,' he said in sardonic comment.

Gina hunted desperately through her mind, but she could find no viable argument to plead her cause. She heaved a defeated sigh and repeated without any hope at all, 'Never for the money.'

Liam carefully sat the doll down on the table and lifted disbelieving eyes. 'But you would...if you had to,' he suggested softly.

In sheer desperation she answered, 'Only with you. Because I loved you.'

For one heart-lifting moment she thought she had reached him. The need to believe blazed from his eyes, but, as quickly as it had flared, it was abruptly snuffed out. 'No! I have to be sure this time.'

'I'll prove it to you!' Gina cried. 'I'll show you what I feel for you!' She snatched up the papers in front of her, crumpled them into a ball and threw them on the floor. 'You say that they're worth a fortune. I don't want it. I won't take a penny of it.'

His eyes narrowed into hard slits. 'Yes, you will. You won't deprive your child of the advantages it can give her. Jim would have wanted his daughter to have everything, and I insist that you take the money for her, if not for yourself.'

'Don't be such a hypocrite!' Gina yelled at him, leaping to her feet and banging her hands on the table in vehement protest. 'You hated Jim! You told me so yourself! You wanted to kill him!'

Liam's head jerked up, his eyes flashing contempt. 'That was the measure of my passion for you, Gina! If it had been any other man taking you as his wife, do you think I would have let him? Jim was the dearest person in my life, closer than a brother, and I get no satisfaction from his death, even though it releases you.'

He paced up and down in the agitation of long-suppressed emotions. 'You couldn't even begin to understand unless you'd been through those cold-hearted welfare homes with us. Deserted by mothers...and fathers...families that didn't care. I told myself I didn't care, they taught me not to care...but Jim did. Jim longed for a home life. We shared everything in those years. Adventure... money...fears...hopes...dreams....'

His voice trailed off into a silence that conjured up the essence of a friendship that Gina had always resented. And again she felt shamed by the judgements she had made.

Liam heaved a deep sigh and shook his head in pain. 'I would have sworn that nothing could come between us.' His eyes turned to her in longing and regret. 'But you did, Gina. You did. I couldn't bear to see you with him, and I had to go away. There was nothing else I could do...for Jim or myself.'

'He missed you,' Gina murmured, remembering how often Jim had talked of Liam, knowing she spoke the truth as she added, 'He missed the excitement you brought into his life.'

Liam turned away with an anguished groan, and Gina felt more wretched than ever. She had thought Liam without feeling, totally selfish, caring for no one but himself. And she had called *him* blind! It seemed that she had never understood anything about him. Nothing at all. But at least she was learning now, and she would never, never judge him harshly again. She had done him so many injuries that it was a miracle he was even with her now.

'I'm sorry I came between you,' she said softly. 'I didn't set out to, Liam.'

He swung around, his face drawn with a loneliness that smote her heart. 'It wasn't your fault. I don't blame you for that, Gina.'

'I was more or less an orphan too, you know,' she said, wanting his understanding for the choice she had made six years ago. 'My mother and grandmother were dead. My father had deserted us when I was a little child. I was very lonely when I met Jim. He knew...he saw...and he cared, Liam.'

'Yes, he would,' Liam murmured.

It encouraged her. 'It meant a great deal to me. I could depend on Jim's love. He showed it to me in so many endearing ways, and I knew he would never walk out on me as my father had. That was very important to me in those days. I didn't realise until after we were married that Jim depended so much on me.'

'I know, Gina,' Liam said quietly, and for the first time she felt empathy coming from him in a soft, gentle wave. 'I used to pick up after Jim, fix things for him. He was never any good at coping by himself, but he always meant to.' He sighed. 'Jim and his good intentions.'

'Yes,' Gina said bitterly, then shook her head in guilty shame. 'Jim had promised me he'd take out insurance because of the gliding. I shouldn't have blamed him for not doing it. I knew well enough that he let things like that slide on and on. I should have followed it up myself. It didn't matter at first, and wouldn't have mattered at all if the problem with Debbie's eyes hadn't developed. But then...'

She sighed and lifted apologetic eyes to Liam. 'And I'm sorry for being bitter with you on your yacht, just because you'd made money.'

Liam stiffened. The flow of empathy was instantly cut off. Gina wished she had bitten off her tongue before it had raised the sore point of Liam's wealth.

'You could have told me about Debbie that day in the office,' he said in a sharply critical tone. 'I would have given you the money for her operation right then and there. For Jim's sake alone, I would give his daughter anything within my power.'

She made a helpless gesture of appeal. 'How was I to know?'

His eyes hardened. 'You know it now, Gina. And all you have to do is sign that paper.'

He bent down, picked up the crumpled ball and straightened out the pages. He thrust them in front of her and placed the pen on top of them.

Gina instantly panicked. It was a trap. He was testing her in some insidious way, and if she signed she would lose him. 'No! We'll get by without your money, Liam. Debbie's not handicapped any more,' she said vehemently.

His face tightened. 'Don't be so selfish!'

The accusation drew blood. 'I've never been selfish with Debbie! Never!'

'Only your pride is stopping you from signing this paper,' he retaliated with another whiplash. 'Those shares are being given to you without any strings whatsoever. Free and clear. If you don't take them, you'll be deliberately disadvantaging your daughter. And I call that selfish.'

Tears of frustration burnt her eyes as she grabbed the papers and sat down to write. 'Damn you, Liam Shannon! Damn you! Damn you! Damn you!' she cried as she scrawled her signature on the crossed line and hurled the pen across the room in bitter defeat. He would never believe her now. Never forgive her. Never...

'Thank you.' He smiled as he picked up the papers. 'Cheer up! The problems are solved! After tomorrow, just contact Mr Jepherson. All you have to do is tell him how many shares you want to sell.'

He folded the papers, slid them back into their envelope and tucked it away in his pocket. 'I'll be going now,' he said, a wicked glint of amusement lightening his eyes. 'Having been so comprehensively cursed by you, Gina, all I can look forward to is an upturn in my fortune over the next sixty days.'

'Sixty days?' she repeated, dull-witted from the weight of hopelessness that burdened her mind and heart.

'Have you forgotten already?' he mocked. 'I'll be back in sixty days for your answer. To whether you will marry me. Meanwhile, enjoy your new wealth. Say goodbye to Debbie for me.'

He was already at the door into the hallway before Gina could unscramble her emotions enough to call after him. 'Liam!'

He turned, a look of cynical enquiry on his face.

Gina hastily swallowed her pride. 'What are you going to do...meanwhile?'

His shoulders lifted and fell in a careless shrug. 'I could take up Jim's challenge and have a try at the long-distance gliding record. If I kill myself, Gina, it will at least remove the pressure from you of having make a decision.'

'Please don't!' she begged, rising from her chair in agitation.

His mouth quirked. 'Don't what?'

'Don't go gliding. You...you could die. Like Jim.'

'And you wouldn't want that, Gina?'

'No, no, no!' she said in frantic impatience with his mockery.

The sardonic quirk grew into a musing smile. 'That's the first bit of encouragement I've had in all the years I've known you. So I'll do something else instead.'

He looked at her then with hard intensity, as if he was re-imprinting her on his memory. 'You know, Gina, we feel the same way about a lot of things,' he said softly. 'I need the security of knowing you won't walk out on me. Keep well until we meet again, my dear.'

He lifted his hand in a brief salute, then headed for the front door.

CHAPTER EIGHT

GINA checked the impulse to run after Liam. He would surely treat any attempt to stop him with suspicion. She had already done all she could to convince him he was wrong. And failed. He had left her no other choice but to let him go. For now.

Gina's hands clenched as a fierce determination swept through her. She would get Liam back. She didn't know how. But she would. If it was the last thing she ever did, she would make him love her again. The sixty days he had stipulated felt like a lifelong sentence of banishment, but the time would pass. And then...

Then she would be four months pregnant... and Liam would think she was accepting him for the child's sake!

Gina groaned in sheer anguish and slumped back down on the chair, despair draining the fighting strength she needed so desperately. She reached across the table for the doll that Liam had toyed with, a beautiful doll with long, wavy black hair, its arms lifted... waiting... asking... wanting...

The tears had dried on her cheeks, but Gina was still holding the doll when the front door was opened and Debbie came pelting into the kitchen.

Her little face fell in disappointment. 'Is Liam gone?'

Gina managed a semblance of a smile. 'Yes, he had to go, Debbie. He said to tell you goodbye.'

'Is he coming back soon?' her daughter pressed anxiously.

Gina put a reassuring arm around her shoulders, aware that the tense scene between herself and Liam could only have been disturbing to the little girl. 'Not for a while, Debbie. We have to wait sixty days.'

'I can count to sixty,' Debbie said with satisfaction, then threw Gina a delighted smile. 'You've got the doll that Liam said looked like you, Mummy. And he said I'm as beautiful as you, even though my hair is all shaved off.'

A huge lump of emotion choked any speech for a moment, and Gina rubbed her cheek over the short black fuzz on her daughter's head. 'You hair will grow soon enough, Debbie,' she said huskily. 'When Liam comes back, it will be all curls.'

Esme's hand fell on her shoulder and gently squeezed. 'Are you all right, Gina?'

'Yes. Fine.' She dragged her gaze up to Esme's anxious face and tried an apologetic smile. 'I'm sorry for worrying you. I should have explained about Liam.'

Esme's face quickly recomposed itself into a look of arch enquiry. 'Well, I thought I could put two and two together, but when I left here, four didn't appear to be a happy answer.'

'Maybe not,' Gina sighed. 'But it's the only answer. He doesn't believe me, but I do love him, Esme. I didn't know it myself until the night . . .'

The bitter-sweet memory brought another rush of tears to her eyes.

'The night he gave you the money for Debbie's operation,' Esme finished for her.

'You guessed...'

Esme rolled her eyes. 'It wasn't hard. I would have accepted five hundred dollars for my painting, but he insisted on paying me five thousand. And this afternoon... I thought it was love at first sight with him and Debbie, and I was feeling so pleased. I could hardly believe it when he turned on you so...' She shook her head in pained disapproval.

'It's a long story, Esme.' Gina nodded to her daughter, who was all ears. 'And I think it had better wait.'

With her usual quick understanding, Esme contained her curiosity, but Debbie was not so easily diverted. She chattered on about Liam non-stop. Liam had told her all about her daddy; Liam had been everywhere and knew about everything; and by the time Gina finally put her daughter to bed for the night, it was painfully obvious that Liam had achieved the status of some wonderful demi-god in Debbie's mind.

Gina went back downstairs to Esme with one certainty in her mind. Debbie would only be too delighted to accept Liam as her stepfather. And Gina was doubly conscious of having underestimated Liam's character. Not only his character, but the very nature of the man, which she had distorted out of all reality to justify her prejudice against him.

Even as she told the whole story to Esme, Gina kept receiving new insights about Liam, some prompted by Esme's perceptive comments, others evolving from the different way her knowledge of the facts now fitted into the overall picture.

'He is an extraordinary man!' Esme observed with awed respect and admiration when Gina had finished outlining the terms Liam had laid down for his ultimate proposal of marriage. She patted Gina's hand. 'And don't you worry, dear. Only a man who loves you very deeply would go to such lengths.'

'"Obsessed" was the word Liam used, Esme,' Gina drily reminded her, then took a slow, deep breath to steady her nerves before revealing the last unavoidable truth. 'There's something else. And I don't know how Liam is going to react to it. I...couldn't tell him this afternoon.'

'Gina, I doubt there's anything you could tell him that would be worse than what he's already been through,' Esme said in sympathetic encouragement.

'I'm pregnant, Esme,' Gina blurted out on a wave of inner anguish. 'I'm seven weeks pregnant, and I'm afraid Liam won't believe it's his child. And he might think I want to marry him because...because I want a father for my baby.'

With her remarkable ability to absorb and deal with any reality, Esme perceived the problem and attacked it. 'Haven't you managed without a father for Debbie? And with all the money he's given you, there's no reason in the world to marry Liam unless you love him,' she argued convincingly. 'Liam

Shannon is too smart not to see that. And as for thinking that the child might not be his, I'll soon set him straight on that point!'

Gina felt somewhat cheered by Esme's sublime confidence, but she could not fully share it. Liam's view of her was still distorted. Had she convinced him this afternoon that she had not been in any man's bed but his?

Her hand lifted and spread protectively over her stomach. Somehow, there had to be a way to make everything work out right. If only Liam would accept that the child she was carrying was his, Gina knew he would want it. The way he treated Debbie showed how deeply he would care. But would he ever believe that she loved him?

The days passed all too slowly, each one carrying its burden of anxious uncertainties over the future. Gina felt continually queasy with her pregnancy, and was grateful that she did not have to hold a job, but time hung all the more heavily. Too much time to think . . . to regret . . . to worry.

She contacted Mr Jepherson and sold the NECSEC shares Liam had thrust upon her. Mr Jepherson was most respectful. His remarkably changed manner towards her was Gina's first taste of the power of money, and she suddenly understood why Liam was so cynical about it. However, she took Debbie shopping for new clothes, and had the pleasure of knowing she did not have to keep to a tight budget.

Another less fleeting and warmer pleasure was in seeing Esme's joy in Bruno Vincente's company.

The rotund little Italian called by every day, ostensibly to encourage Esme's painting and confirm arrangements for her gallery showing; but their conversation was a stream of glowing approval of each other, and their eyes were full of mutual and adoring admiration.

One afternoon, Gina and Debbie came home from the supermarket to find Esme in a delirium of happiness, having just painted the most extraordinary picture.

'It's called Pistachio!' she informed Debbie.

'What's that?' Debbie asked curiously.

'Italian ice-cream. With lots of lovely surprises in it,' said Esme with irrepressible smugness.

Gina could not help herself. The laughter bubbled out of her throat and, after one surprised look, Esme's great rollicking laugh burst out too, expressing a boundless joy with life.

'He says he loves me!' Esme confided after Debbie had gone to bed that night.

'Who wouldn't love you, Esme?' Gina assured her.

'He says he wants to take me to Italy with him to meet his family,' Esme continued in a kind of surprised wonder.

'I'm sure they'll love you, too.'

'But I said I couldn't go until I see you and Debbie settled with Liam.'

Gina sighed, unable to feel so certain about that eventuality. 'Esme, you've done so much for Debbie and me; please put your own interests first now.

Whatever happens between Liam and me...well, that's our problem.'

'Nonsense!' declared Esme. 'I refuse to miss out on your wedding. And that won't be long after my gallery showing, anyway.'

And Esme wouldn't budge from that decision, despite the fact that the opening date for the exhibition of her paintings was only a couple of weeks away.

The next fortnight passed a little more easily for Gina, due to the distraction that Esme and Bruno provided. They were in a fever of excited activity leading up to the World Première, as Bruno insisted on calling Esme's introduction to Sydney's art world. Glossy catalogues and invitations were sent to prospective buyers, the paintings were hung in the gallery, cases of Moët et Chandon champagne ordered. Bruno predicted a scintillating success.

Unfortunately when the great day came, Gina was far from well. The morning sickness did not abate at all, and she felt dizzy and nauseous even as she forced herself to dress for the evening. She wanted to crawl into bed and lie there, but she couldn't let Esme down on the night of her triumph. She hoped there were a few handy chairs around the showrooms.

Debbie looked absolutely beautiful in her new clothes. Her hair had grown into a pretty cap of black curls, and her eyes positively danced with the excitement of being part of such a grown-up, important occasion. Esme insisted it was Debbie's night too, since it was her inspiration that had led to the 'great leap forward'!

When they arrived at the gallery, it seemed that Bruno's organisation had certainly aroused a great deal of interest in Esme's work, for the rooms were overflowing with people. The paintings were beautifully lit and displayed, and Gina felt that everyone had to recognise Esme's unique talent.

'Liam!' Debbie squealed, and went charging off through the crowd, leaving Gina rooted to the spot as her eyes sought him out and her heart leapt into overdrive.

She caught his laughing face as he hoisted Debbie into the air, and never had he looked so devastatingly handsome, nor so intensely desirable. Gina's head spun from the sheer pleasure of seeing him, and a deep, clawing need added its nauseous momentum to an already churning stomach. She needed to sit down quite desperately, but there were no vacant chairs nearby, and Liam was coming towards her... Liam, holding Debbie in his arms, smiling at her daughter, calling her sweetheart.

'Gina...' It was a wary nod of acknowledgment, his eyes making an excruciatingly slow appraisal of the rich green silk dress she had been tempted into buying for the occasion. The semi-fitted style was graceful and elegant, and so cunningly cut that it showed off Gina's figure to every advantage and hid her extra inches around the waist. It also looked every bit as expensive as it was.

Liam's mouth curved into an ironic half-smile. 'Wealth becomes you, my dear.'

'I'm glad you're here, Liam.' She spoke from the heart, but the words came out faintly, strangled by too much emotion. She fiercely wished she had worn old rags.

'I have an interest in the art world at the moment,' he said carelessly.

Too carelessly! Gina's intuition pricked to full alert. Liam was masking his true feelings. Protecting himself. He had shown himself vulnerable to her once. It was unlikely that he would do that again until he was completely sure of her.

'I've just promised to buy Debbie her choice of Esme's paintings,' he continued blithely. 'Would you like to tour the rooms with us, or would you prefer your own company?'

Despite his relaxed demeanour, Gina could feel the tension emanating from him—a tight coil of expectancy that was being repressed with iron control.

She wasn't at all sure how far her legs would take her, but she couldn't afford to admit to any weakness. Not only would Liam interpret the declining of his invitation as a personal rejection, but Gina couldn't bear to miss out on the opportunity of being with him.

'I'll come with you,' she said quickly, hoping for a chance to convince him of her love.

Liam raised a querying eyebrow. 'I assure you, Debbie's perfectly safe with me.'

'I know.' Her eyes battled against the hard defence in his and lost. 'Don't you want me with you?' she asked bleakly.

He shrugged. 'The decision is entirely up to you.'

He set off with Debbie, and Gina fell into step beside him, her legs wobbling uncertainly and her mind seeking frantically for words that might help break through Liam's armour of apparent indifference.

He slanted her a taunting smile. 'Have you worked out how you'll rationalise it to yourself when you reject my offer of marriage?'

A wave of misery weakened Gina further. He had reason for his pessimism. She had rationalised herself into marrying Jim instead of seeing her mistake and accepting Liam. And now...was Liam ever going to believe her? She had to make some positive move to convince him he was wrong about her.

'I know I was a fool not to face up to what I felt for you all those years ago, but please don't keep making me pay for it, Liam,' she begged. Her eyes desperately sought some softening in his. 'I love you. I don't want to wait another twenty days. I want to be with you. I need you.'

Her voice was barely a whisper of yearning, but it stopped him mid-step. He turned and faced her, his eyes wary but no longer hard, and, having won his undivided attention, Gina pressed on, anxious for him to keep listening, even if it was with only a half-open mind.

'When I was married to Jim, did money ever replace what you wanted, Liam?'

His face tightened and his eyes seemed to darken with an intense watchfulness that wound Gina's nerves into painful knots.

'Money's not worth a damn!' he answered shortly.

'That's what I feel!' Gina argued. 'It's nothing when you're forced to live without the person you love.'

Having recklessly drawn on the last of her strength to inject vehement conviction into her voice, Gina had nothing left with which to fight the sick rebellion of her body. Her face went cold and clammy as the blood drained away in a relentlessly receding tide. Her head swam in darkening circles. Her stomach cramped. Her legs lost all substance. She clutched wildly at Liam's arm, her eyes blindly appealing for support.

'Gina!' The harsh urgency in his voice echoed in her ears. An arm came around her, clamping her tightly against him. 'Down, Debbie! Quick! I have to look after your mummy.'

She vaguely felt Debbie's small body slithering past hers. 'Mummy? Will I get Esme?' her small voice piped anxiously.

Gina was beyond speech. She was vaguely aware that Liam was holding her at last, that it was his warmth and strength supporting her, but she was too ill to take any pleasure in the circumstances.

'Gina! Tell me what's wrong!'

The sharp demand penetrated the gathering darkness, pushing it back momentarily. 'Liam . . .'

She tried to rally—aware of a terrible need to reach him—but the effort required produced the opposite effect and she slipped into unconsciousness.

'...the baby.' Esme's anxious voice cut through the cotton-wool that seemed to have blanketed Gina's mind.

'My God!' Liam sounded appalled, pained. 'Look after Debbie, will you, Esme?'

'What about Gina?'

'I'll get a doctor to her as soon...as soon...God damn it! I'll buy a doctor!'

She was being carried...held gently, carefully, lovingly...and somehow it didn't matter that the world was spinning around her. Liam held her safe.

CHAPTER NINE

'GINA ... Gina ...' Liam's lips were pressed to her forehead, warming her cold skin with the passionate whisper of her name and soft, yearning kisses. His hand gently stroked her hair away from her temples. He held her half-cradled across his lap.

As Gina slowly regained full consciousness she became aware that her legs were stretched out along the back seat of a car, and the car was moving. She fought down a wave of nausea and pushed her eyes open. Her hand plucked weakly at his jacket.

'Liam ...' Her voice was a husky croak.

Instantly his hand moved to tenderly caress her cheek, and his eyes anxiously met hers to reassure. 'It's all right. I'll take care of you. You'll never have to worry about another thing. Rest easy, my love.'

Gina's heart pumped a massive surge of life through her body. Had Liam believed her? Was it all right? She hastily moistened her throat. 'I love you, Liam.'

Anguished eyes searched hers, unable to believe.

'We're going to have a baby,' she added softly, hopefully.

His face contorted with raging conflicts. 'Why didn't you tell me, Gina? Esme said you knew you were pregnant that afternoon when I came to see if there was any chance left for us. You knew, and you didn't tell me!'

Her hope sank into the mire of misunder-standing that had plagued them right from the start. 'Whatever I do is wrong,' she sighed, too sick to fight any more accusations.

'No!' He held her closer and rubbed his cheek over her hair as he spoke in pained little bursts. 'Not you, Gina. Me. Forcing, forcing, forcing. I'm still doing it and I don't mean to. I hardly know what I'm saying. I don't know how to ask you to forgive me.'

He pulled back enough to meet her eyes with a tortured plea. 'I wouldn't have walked away if you'd told me, Gina. I'd never have left you ... without even any means to contact me,' he added in an agony of guilt. 'You know that, don't you?'

'Yes,' she whispered. 'But if I'd told you ... I thought you might see it as some form of emotion-al blackmail ... to trap you into a marriage where you would never be sure of anything, Liam. And you thought badly enough of me as it was. I didn't want you to ... to stand by me, Liam, with the baby clouding everything between us.'

'But to suffer it alone, while I ...' He shook his head in bitter self-condemnation. 'Esme told me how sick you've been. I wanted you to trust me with your life ... your future ... and Debbie's, too ... and I've proven in the worst possible way that I don't deserve you. You must have been hoping and wishing for a miscarriage ...'

She shut her eyes tight and turned her head away from him, utterly repulsed that Liam should even imagine such a possibility.

'Please...just tell me what you want!' he rasped. 'If you can't bear to have my child, I'll understand, Gina. I was so horribly wrong about your work, and you begged me not to take you, but I selfishly ignored whatever you said. I forced myself upon you and...'

'No!' She opened her eyes, reached up and touched his mouth, silencing his terrible outpouring. 'You didn't force me, Liam. Only at the beginning. I really wanted you...wanted us to make love,' she told him truthfully.

'No...no...how could you love me then? You only gave into me because of the money for Debbie.' His tortured words groaned past the prison of her fingers.

She moved her hand to stroke his cheek, needing to impress her sincerity on him. 'Our baby was conceived out of love...from me, if not from you, Liam. At first I fought you because you thought that I'd sold myself to other men, but you made me forget that hurt...and Debbie. There was only you...only you, Liam.'

'Gina, please... I know I said terrible things...unforgivable. I was mad. But mad from love of you and waiting so long...wanting so much...'

His arms tightened in a convulsive need to press her closer, and he rubbed his cheek over her hair in an agony of longing. 'Just let me take care of

you, Gina. I won't ask any more than that of
you...ever again. You and Debbie...and our child.
All the love I have in my heart—it's for you ... and
any extension of you...'

The limousine pulled up at the Regent Hotel.
Although Gina protested that she was not about to
faint again, Liam insisted on carrying her up to his
suite, where he very gently laid her on the bed, removed her shoes, and covered her with blankets.
He telephoned immediately for a doctor, demanding a gynaecologist—the best—to be sent to
his suite with a minimum of delay...the cost was
immaterial!

Gina could not deny that she still felt unwell, but
she did not think she required the services of a
specialist, and rather self-consciously said so. Liam,
however, was adamant on the point, his whole demeanour clearly distraught over the situation.

'We've got to know if there's something wrong.
If...' He stopped pacing the floor and sat on the
bed beside her, taking her hand and fondling it in
an agitated fashion as his eyes begged her forgiveness. 'Gina, if you don't want my child...if
you want...'

Her heart contracted in savage pain. 'Is that what
you want, Liam?'

'There's nothing I want more than to have...'
He shook his head, anguished by the decision. 'But
I must consider you! I've done nothing else but
push what I've wanted on to you...'

'That's not true!' Gina protested sharply. 'You
saved Debbie's eyesight and...'

'At what price, Gina?' he retorted with a curl of self-contempt. 'Making you pregnant with my child?'

'I *love* you, Liam,' she said fiercely. 'Even if you never married me, I would want your child. At least I would have some part of you.'

'Gina...' Hope flickered through the dark despair in his eyes.

'I love you,' she repeated with all the yearning in her soul. 'Please believe me, Liam.'

'Oh...God!'

Gina wasn't sure if the taut expulsion of breath was a prayer or an oath, but she had little time to think about it. Liam gathered her up, clutching her head against the thundering beat of his heart.

'Tell me this is real! Tell me this isn't another dream!' he cried, tortured beyond bearing. 'All my life I've wanted this...'

'I love you,' she whispered with all the aching need in her own heart, and she slid her arms around his waist, pressing the reality of her desire to hold on to him for ever.

'Gina...' It was the spent sigh of a storm that had left a long, ravaged trail in its wake. Liam's chest slowly expanded and held the indrawn breath, as if he dared not let it go for fear it would subtly alter the magical truth of this critical moment.

'Can you forgive me all the wasted years, Liam?' Gina softly pleaded.

He laughed with a joyous release that rippled through his entire body, and his face shone with an exultant happiness as he gently laid her back on the pillows. 'For this alone have I lived. And the only life that has any meaning begins now,' he said huskily, and kissed her with a tenderness that bordered on veneration.

Again and again his lips came down to meet hers with a depth of emotion that was beyond the passion of sexual need or desire. He softly stroked her face and her hair in a way that made her feel infinitely precious to him. His eyes worshipped her. His mouth held the sweet curve of wondrous contentment.

This stunning revelation of all-consuming love made Gina feel more humble than she had ever felt in her life. She understood now the explosive violence she had always sensed in Liam. It was the violence he had been driven to inflict upon himself in order to repress and contain what he felt for her. With her unreserved acceptance of him, the nerve-tearing tension had finally been dissolved, giving way to an uninhibited expression of a personal commitment that Gina could only hope she would be worthy of.

The doctor arrived. He gave Gina a thorough examination, then questioned her extensively about her morning sickness and diet. He particularly asked if she had been under any physical stress, and frowned heavily when Gina denied any such thing.

'She has been suffering a great deal of emotional distress,' Liam informed him promptly. 'Would that have any bearing on it?'

'That could do it. It alters hormonal levels, Mr Shannon. In these cases, the best thing is complete bed-rest and relaxation. No physical exertion. No upsets. But if there is any further problem, your wife will need to go on a course of injections. Better to avoid it if we can.' He turned gravely to Gina. 'You must let me know immediately if anything out of the usual occurs... pain... spotting...'

'Yes, Doctor,' she agreed quickly, determined not to risk a miscarriage.

'She will get every care, Doctor,' Liam assured him.

The gynaecologist departed, well recompensed, but although Gina was relieved to know that there was no serious problem with her pregnancy, Liam did not exude the same confidence.

'Promise me you'll stay here and not worry about anything, Gina,' he demanded anxiously, gathering her into his embrace to reinforce his concern for her. 'I'll call Esme. She can bring Debbie to visit you. I'll make all the arrangements necessary. There's a telephone in the bathroom as well as by the bed. No matter where you are, you can always call for help.'

'But won't you be here?' Gina asked, bewildered by his instructions.

'My darling, I wish I could stay at your side every minute, but... a small thing... the smallest trifle... nevertheless, I must do it now.' He smiled. 'But ahead of anything else, first thing I have to do tomorrow morning is obtain a special licence for us to get married.'

She laughed at the wonderful impatience that implied, then curled her arms teasingly around his neck, her eyes promising him everything as she spoke. 'In that case, I'll do whatever you say.'

His smile turned lop-sided. 'Don't tempt me, darling. I think I've just swapped one form of torture for another; until, of course, the doctor says otherwise.'

But his eyes assured her that it was a torture he didn't mind at all. He kissed her very lightly, then a shade more urgently, and finally with a pent-up passion that left them both breathing raggedly and wanting far more of each other.

Liam dragged himself out of Gina's embrace and snatched up the room-service menu from the bedside table. 'Food!' he commanded with an edge of desperation. 'Got to look after you and the baby. Must be something that you can eat. Make you feel better...'

He concentrated hard on the menu, reading out each item and exaggerating every possible bit of nutritious value to such a wild extreme that Gina relaxed into laughter again. He heaved a sigh and grinned at her. 'I've got to do something to make you behave responsibly.'

Her eyes twinkled back at him, happy beyond belief. 'I'll do my best to eat whatever you order.'

With typical extravagance, Liam ordered a banquet, and to Gina's surprise her queasy stomach co-operated very well, settling quite comfortably under the food Liam persuaded her to eat. She felt a great deal better by the time the meal was over, and Liam glowed with smug satisfaction.

'You see? I'm good for you. You need me,' he told her.

'Yes,' she agreed, smiling her own satisfaction. 'And I love you, too.'

'Gina . . .' He threaded his fingers through hers, and his eyebrows knotted anxiously as he searched for the words he wanted. 'I've made so many bad moves. I don't deserve to have you . . . the way I've gone about it . . . all wrong. But I never stopped believing, in my heart, that we were meant to belong to each other . . . if I could only make it happen.'

He gave an apologetic little smile. 'I guess I wasn't brought up to the niceties of life. All I ever knew was fighting to get what I wanted, because I sure as hell knew that no one was ever going to give it to me on a platter. But you shame me very deeply with your giving, Gina. I promise you, in future, I'll do my best to live up to it.'

'Liam, you are a giving person,' Gina protested.

'Not like you,' he insisted. 'But one thing I've always done, Gina . . . when I give my word, I keep it. You can trust me with your life, Gina. And with Debbie's. And with any children we have. I swear to you, I'll always look after you and do my best to keep you happy. Please say you believe me.'

'I do.' She smiled, wanting this last shadow lifted from their relationship, and certain that Liam meant every word. 'I do trust you, Liam,' she sighed happily, and drew him down on to the pillow next to her.

The night was pure bliss, even though they did not make love. Gina lay contentedly in Liam's arms, basking in the tender caring of his love for her, knowing that for the rest of her life this man was hers. It gave her a feeling of fulfilment that was beautifully complete. They did not need any physical intimacy to prove they belonged to each other. They were together in a sense that joined their lives for ever.

For the first time in many weeks, Gina was not sick the next morning. Nevertheless, Liam insisted on serving her breakfast in bed. He stacked pillows behind her and Gina sat there in state, clothed in one of the thick white full-length bathrobes provided by the hotel, and wearing a smile that danced continually at the man who was pampering her with so much love.

The curtains of the corner suite were drawn back to reveal a fantastic panorama of the harbour, and it was a sparkling blue day that gave a vivid sharpness to all its magnificent features: the majestic span of the Harbour Bridge, the gleaming sails of the Opera House roof, the ferries streaming across the water to Circular Quay, the historic battlements of Fort Denison, the endless fascination of all its coves and inlets.

Gina had no reluctance whatsoever in giving Liam another promise to stay in bed before he left her, but apparently he was not prepared to take any chances that she might change her mind. Within minutes of his departure from the suite, a member of the hotel staff arrived with an armful of magazines and a selection of paperbacks that were currently on the best-seller list.

Morning tea was sent up without any request from her. The roses arrived next—a bowl positively brimming with two dozen of the most beautiful red blooms. Then Esme and Debbie came in, bubbling with excitement.

'We're staying here, too!' Debbie announced, barely giving Gina a kiss of greeting before rushing to the windows to take in the view.

'Liam booked us into adjoining rooms,' Esme informed, beaming with pleasure at such unaccustomed luxury. 'And all my paintings have sold!' she added in delighted triumph. 'I'm rich! I'm rich! I'm rich!'

For the next hour Gina was regaled with the unqualified success of Esme's exhibition at the gallery; the amazing perspicacity of Bruno Vincente's superb judgement; the wonderful write-up that the art critics had given her work in the newspapers; and, not last nor least, her happiness that Gina and Liam had solved all their differences.

Their conversation was interrupted by the delivery of a pile of elegant boxes containing the most exquisite nightie and négligé sets Gina had ever seen—the softest of fine silk and satin with fabulous lace inserts, and in almost every colour to delight the eye: white, peach, misty green, blue, red, black. Esme and Debbie couldn't lift them out of their tissue-paper wrappings fast enough, breathless with admiration at the sheer feminine glamour of the garments.

'That man is bursting with love for you, Gina,' Esme declared.

'Put the green one on, Mummy,' Debbie urged.

Gina obliged her daughter and felt almost like a movie queen as she paraded the beautiful gown and matching négligé in front of Debbie, who clapped with delight.

'I think the idea is to keep you happy in bed,' Esme said archly. 'And you'd better get back there before Liam walks in, or we'll all be in trouble.'

A ruinously tempting luncheon was sent up to the suite. 'Liam is spoiling me rotten,' Gina observed, finding an appetite that had totally deserted her in the last few months.

'I like being spoilt rotten,' Debbie enthused with eager innocence.

'Me, too,' said Esme, eyeing the delicious food with approving relish.

After lunch, Esme insisted that Gina had to rest throughout the afternoon, and she took Debbie off to her own room for a nap. Gina did not sleep, but she weaved wonderful dreams about the future, and when Liam finally returned, the welcome she gave him almost shattered the restraint they had agreed upon for the sake of the baby.

Liam triumphantly produced a marriage form for Gina to sign, demanded a report on everything she had done, observed that the green nightie was exceptionally becoming, decided he had splendid taste in choosing clothes for her and would make a point of doing more of it in future . . . in Rome, in Paris, in London, in New York . . .

Debbie joined them for the evening meal in their suite, and Liam's manner with the little girl showed Gina precisely why Esme had been so approving of him on the afternoon that he had brought the Christmas tree. He was wonderful with Debbie—loving, attentive, amusing, effortlessly making her feel very special to him. Debbie adored him.

Esme came to collect Debbie for the night. She had dined with Bruno in the elegant Kable's Restaurant on the first floor, and the Italian accompanied her into the suite, kindly enquiring after Gina's health, then tactfully standing aside while Esme and Debbie chatted on for a few minutes.

Gina was giving Debbie one last hug when she noticed the two men talking together. Bruno's face had lost all trace of its geniality, and he was concentrating intensely on what Liam was saying. Liam's voice was so low that his words did not carry, but hie expression had assumed the hard, ruthless air of authority that reminded Gina of their meeting in the hotel lobby three months ago. A business contact, Liam had said, and she idly wondered what business they had done together. And for so long!

'Tomorrow,' Bruno said on a decisive note.

Liam nodded, then recomposed his face into a smile for Esme, who had stepped over to the Italian's side, taking his arm with uninhibited pleasure. Liam collected Debbie from Gina and saw them all out of the suite. When he returned to Gina's side, she forgot all about Liam's connection with Bruno, and luxuriated in his totally distracting absorption with her.

Liam had miraculously arranged for their marriage to take place in ten days' time. He told her that his yacht—their yacht—was already on its way to the Mediterranean and, if she wanted to, they could have a long, long honeymoon cruising around all the beautiful islands there. Provided, of course, that Gina stayed well.

It was not until after breakfast the next morning that Liam broke the news to her. 'Three days. Four at the most, I promise you. And then nothing will ever separate us again,' he assured her. 'But this one last time I must leave you, Gina.'

'But why do you have to go? What do you have to do now?' she pressed, every instinct clamouring to keep him with her at all costs.

He flashed her a dismissive smile. 'A brief business trip, Gina. Nothing for you to worry about.'

She frowned. 'You haven't told me what business you're in, Liam.' She lifted anxious eyes. 'I really don't know much about your present life at all, do I?'

He grinned. 'You're my present life. As for business, I do very well out of my investments.' His grin grew wider. 'Like the NECSEC shares. I've always been lucky, except in what mattered to me most, and now I've even got you. So nothing could possibly go wrong.'

But there a guarded look in his eyes that sent prickles of apprehension down Gina's spine. 'Liam, you haven't taken on anything dangerous like the gun-running you did when...'

He laughed. 'I left those days behind long ago. No, my love, this is eminently respectable. I'm going to make a lot of money, but you mustn't ask about it. Not yet. I want to keep it as a surprise for you. I'll tell you all about it when I get back.'

'Get back from where?' A fearful idea blasted into her mind. 'Liam, I'll never forgive you if you're going gliding.'

He took her in his arms. 'My darling, I assure you I'm not going gliding. It's actually someting you suggested to me, something you'd want. And I can't back out now. I gave my word, and other people are depending on me to carry it out, so I must go. Now please...you are not to distress yourself. Remember the baby. You must be good. And believe me, nothing in the world could stop me from coming back to you.'

'Promise me you'll take care of yourself,' she insisted, still ill at ease, without being able to pinpoint why, but her sixth sense was picking up something that alarmed her, despite Liam's re-assurances. 'If anything happens to you, I'll murder you myself, Liam.'

'Trust me,' he commanded, hugging her tightly, then kissing her as if he was savouring the taste of her for the long hours of absence ahead of him. When he drew back, his eyes held a glitter of intense purpose.

'This will be my last time, my last job, Gina. I'm going to devote the rest of my life to giving you all the pleasure I can think of. But I have to do this first.' He smiled. 'Mind you're ready for me when I return. I want you to have everything your heart desires for the rest of your life.'

He gave her no time for further questions or protests. He was off and away, with a sudden abruptness that left her completely bereft, as if she had lost the most important part of her life.

They had been together—truly together—for such a short time, but the joy of it had been so blissful that Gina knew that, if she ever lost Liam now, her life would be unbearable. He was right. They had always been meant for each other. Nothing could be more right than the love they shared.

And of course she wasn't going to lose him. It was silly of her to even entertain the thought. Liam was only going to be away for three or four days. Just a brief business trip...eminently respectable. He had asked her to trust him and she did. It was stupid to worry...not good for the baby.

Gina snuggled back down on her pillow with a resigned sigh. A surprise for her, Liam had said. Something that she had suggested to him. Gina couldn't remember suggesting anything, but no doubt Liam had thought up something hopelessly extravagant. As lovely as it was to be spoilt rotten, she really would have to impress on him that nothing meant more to her than their being together.

CHAPTER TEN

LIAM did not come back on the third day.

Gina felt very disgruntled. He hadn't told her where he was going and she didn't know where he was or what he was doing. He hadn't telephoned her once in the three days he had been away, not even to check if their child was behaving itself—which it was, but that was not the point!

Gina, on the other hand, had done exactly what Liam had told her: stayed in bed and not exerted herself in any way. But her mind was mightily exerted on that third night, after she had waited hours and hours for another telephone call that never came. No matter what business was tying up his time, he could surely have taken a few moments to use a telephone . . . at least once. Wasn't he missing her as much as she missed him?

Surprises were all very well, but this was going too far. She realised that Liam had never had anybody to account to before, and she supposed he had to be broken in to the kind of thoughtfulness and consideration that a relationship required, but that didn't really excuse his neglect. And she would tell him so tomorrow.

But when Gina wakened to a bright new morning, the dark thoughts of the previous night were washed away with the excited anticipation of Liam's imminent return to her. She took a long shower, put on the peach nightie, and brightened up her pale face with some judicious make-up. Her hair was still bouncy and shiny from the washing she had given it yesterday in preparation for Liam's homecoming, and she brushed it into a silky ripple of waves.

She propped herself up in bed with magazines spread around her, determined to look exactly how Liam would want her to look. Esme and Debbie came in for a brief morning visit. Esme archly suggested that it was a good day to take Debbie on the ferry to Taronga Park Zoo on the other side of the harbour. Gina was quick to agree.

Her heart leapt excitedly at a knock on the door, until her mind told her it could not be Liam. He would not knock. He had a key. A member of the hotel staff, she reasoned, come to ask if she wanted something done. She opened the door and felt a ripple of surprise when Bruno Vincente presented himself. He had never visited her without Esme in tow.

He came in exuding outlandish excitement, his face glowing rosily, his eyes flashing, his hands expressing a rapid range of emotions. 'You are not to be upset, Gina!' he commanded triumphantly. 'All is well! Only a little trouble that delays Mr Shannon's return, but he will be here for the marriage day without fail. Sonner if possible.'

Gina shook her head in confusion. Liam had been in contact with Bruno Vincente, and not with her? Her mind suddenly cleared as she remembered the two men speaking together the night before Liam left. 'You were involved in this business trip of Liam's?'

'It is why I came to Australia,' Bruno informed her, then bubbled into sheer exultation. 'All these months of planning and now it is done. Ah... success! It is beautiful!'

'What success?' Gina demanded impatiently. 'And why is Liam delayed?'

Bruno controlled himself enough to take her gently by the arm and lead her back to bed. 'Now, you are not to be upset, Gina,' he soothed. 'Mr Shannon expressly forbade it. I am to tell you there is nothing for you to worry about.'

The soothing was a little too much. All sorts of fears ran rampant through Gina's mind. 'What trouble? You said some trouble had delayed Liam.'

'If you lie down and relax, I will tell you,' Bruno promised. 'But you are not to be upset.'

Gina swallowed her frustration with Bruno's fussing and climbed into bed, but every nerve was tingling with apprehension as she schooled her expression to a calmness she was far from feeling.

Bruno smiled approvingly at her. 'You must understand there is no danger now. He is being fixed up. No problem. You are not to worry.'

'Fixed up from what?' Gina almost screamed at him.

Bruno looked troubled. 'A little hurt. He was shot in the shoulder, and... er... concussion. It is best that he does not travel for the time being. But he is all right. You are not to distress yourself about him. He is under a doctor's care in Florida. A good doctor he knows from the past.'

A blaze of excitement wiped out Bruno's momentary concern. 'He did it, Gina! I was told that he was the only man in the world who had any chance of bringing it off. And he did! He did the impossible!'

'At the cost of being hurt,' Gina cut in, a bitter fury engulfing her with the realisation that Liam had lied! People didn't get shot doing respectable business. And going to a doctor that he knew *from the past*! He had told her *those days* were over! And asked her to trust him!

Since she could not vent her anger on Liam, Gina turned it on to Bruno Vincente. It was perfectly plain that the Italian art dealer was up to his ears in this dangerous business. And she had thought him a gentleman!

'What was worth this terrible risk?' she demanded. 'Tell me at once, Bruno!'

The fire of fanaticism burst into his eyes. 'The greatest collection of Fauve and Post-Impressionist paintings ever smuggled out of Russia. Always some of the greatest works were in Moscow and Leningrad where they were not allowed to be reproduced or to be seen. But the Russian Government wanted gold. By devious means they were brought to South America.'

He chuckled, almost delirious with delight. 'They thought they had planned a masterpiece of duplicity. They tried to double-cross us, but Mr Shannon had their measure. He triple-crossed them.

And that was when he got shot. But now...now these great works of art will once more be seen! Roualt, Matisse, Pissarro, Picasso, Dufy, Cézanne...'

'And just where did Liam have to go to do this dirty work?' Gina bored in, totally unimpressed about a few old paintings, and even more furious at Liam's duplicity.

'What a man!' Bruno enthused, obviously thrilled to have been a second-hand part of the operation. 'He brought the collection out through Chile, then on to his yacht and straight through Panama...'

Gina's blood ran cold. 'Isn't there a revolution going on in Chile?'

'Some political troubles,' Bruno agreed carelessly, his eyes shining with the triumph of successful calculation as he added, 'But it allows for corruption in certain places, you see. And of course, where there is a certain amount of chaos, movements are not so easily checked by authorities. Mr Shannon was able to insinuate a network of his old friends...'

As Bruno proudly revealed the details of Liam's plan, Gina's temper rose in seething bursts. Respectable, Liam had said! No word about corruption or subversion or mixing with his old gun-running friends. And he wouldn't dream of gliding! Oh, no! Just a little matter of dodging through a revolution with a load of old contraband. Pitting himself against Russian agents...

'If it was all so beautifully planned, Bruno, how did Liam get hurt?' Gina cut in bitterly.

Bruno frowned. 'There was an unexpected altercation in the dock area as they were shipping the paintings to the yacht. The Russians caught on to the alternative arrangements at the last minute and tried to prevent Mr Shannon from leaving. I understand that he was helping one of his friends into the motor-boat when he was hit...'

'How badly?' Gina's voice rose several decibels.

Bruno waved his hands in quick appeasement. 'It is a neat little hole straight through the shoulder. It completely missed the lung and axillary artery. A mere flesh wound...'

'And the concussion?'

'Er...a slight graze of the scalp. Barely a scratch. A few stitches fixed it. He is well, I assure you.'

He'd been shot twice! Gina didn't need Bruno to spell it out any more clearly. Her fury soared at the reckless disregard of life and limb that these men countenanced for the sake of a few paintings that the world could well do without.

She glared venomously at Bruno. 'You set this up, didn't you? You actually think that this is worth risking Liam's life? To achieve so little?'

Bruno was so entranced with his success that he did not notice the acid note in Gina's questions. His chest puffed out and his hands lifted in a gesture of immense proportions. 'The collection is of great historical importance. I authenticated it myself many months ago on a secret mission to Bolivia.

It is worth at least a hundred million dollars on today's market.'

The incredible figure put Gina off her stride for a moment, but her rage rushed back in full measure. No amount of money or art history was worth Liam's life! His last job, indeed! It could so easily have been his last job in an absolutely fatal sense!

'I'll kill him!' she muttered through furiously clenched teeth.

'What did you say?' Bruno asked, his face still flushed with triumph.

Gina hurled off the bedclothes, leapt to her feet and advanced on him, spitting mad. 'You men! All you ever think of is power and glory! There's not one of you with a grain of common sense in your head! Jim had to go gliding! Liam goes off and risks his life for nothing! And you...you're just as bad, Bruno Vincente, lapping it up from the sidelines!'

He backed away from her, his hands flapping in alarm. 'Gina, you must not upset yourself... everything is all right...'

'I'll upset myself as much as I like. In fact, I'm fighting fit! I've never felt so fighting fit in my life!' She shook her fist at him. 'And I'm ready to fight you right now for what you did!'

He hurriedly stepped back, horrified and flustered by her action. 'I am an art-broker. Mr Shannon struck the deal, and the fee he demanded was extortion. I did not force him into anything.'

'But you love it, don't you? The triumph...the winning!' Gina hurled at him.

'He is safe, Gina. Why are you so...'

'And what if he was dead? Did you think of that, Bruno? Would you still crow over your precious art collection then?'

'But...'

Gina completely lost her temper. 'Get out! You men aren't worth talking to. You're all mad!'

He scuttled off to the door, then turned an anxious face back to her. 'I...er...this is not for general publication, Gina. No one else is to know,' he pleaded.

'Don't worry!' Gina snarled her contempt. 'Your stupid secret business is safe with me. I'm not about to reveal to the world how insane you and Liam are.'

He made an apologetic grimace with his hasty exit. Gina felt like picking up Liam's bowl of roses and throwing it after him. Red roses for love. Love was being with a person when that person needed you, not darting about the world at some art dealer's behest!

Gina paced around the suite, absolutely fuming over Liam's deceit. She had been right all those years ago. Liam Shannon was not a man to trust with her life. He had no respect for his own, and only God knew what he would get up to next!

Jim had told her! Liam lived for excitement. Hadn't he dragged Jim into all sorts of mad scrapes when they were boys? And hadn't he shown how extreme he still was this second time around? Buying those NECSEC shares, abducting her from the office building, forcing her into having sex with him—he would certainly have forced her if she hadn't given in—then giving Debbie a Christmas party in June, passing over all that money, and showering her with gifts!

Bursting with love, Esme called it, but if Liam really cared for her he would have called off this crazy adventure. And how could she love such a madman? She was off her brain to even consider him for a husband and father to her children. He would be a bad influence! A very bad influence indeed! How on earth would she cope if she had a son like him?

Liam had better be back before their wedding day, or she would't marry him at all. That would teach him a much-needed lesson. If he really wanted her so very desperately, then he had better hurry up!

Ever since he had walked into Mr Jepherson's office, Liam had been calling the shots in their relationship. Not any more, Gina vowed. She wouldn't stand for this sweeping around like a modern-day buccaneer ever again. If he wanted to be her husband, he could learn to behave himself. Like any other ordinary human being.

With that resolution set in mental concrete, Gina waited through the next few days, presenting a perfectly calm façade to Esme and Debbie, and even shining up a mood of happy anticipation for Liam's delayed return.

The gynaecologist called by at the end of the week. The medical check was most satisfactory. Fighting fit, the doctor declared. Any danger of a miscarriage was over. Then, with an approving smile, he added that she looked positively blooming with good health after the week's rest. Of course, he wasn't to know that Gina's adrenalin was running high, and the sparkle in her eyes was not entirely due to approaching motherhood. Gina didn't bother enlightening him.

The message came the day before they were to be married. 'Home tonight,' it said. 'All my love, Liam.' No apology, no explanation, no definite hour, just—'Home tonight.' Gina gnashed her teeth over it and planned her own little campaign.

She dressed in the red nightie. She brushed her hair until it crackled with electricity. In fact, her whole body felt as if it was crackling with electricity. She ordered herself a bottle of champagne, a cold seafood platter, put on the glamorous red négligé, then draped herself on one of the green leather sofas near the windows. And waited!

Eight o'clock...nine o'clock...ten... Gina had no difficulty in passing the time. Her mind tumbled over with all the pertinent things she was going to say to Liam. She rehearsed the telling lines over and over, finding a great deal of satisfaction in perfecting them for their ultimate impact.

When she heard the key turning the lock, her heart entirely misbehaved itself and, to Gina's absolute disgust, she had to harness all her will-power to quell the treacherous impulse of her feet to leap up and run to a man who deserved the utmost censure. She took a last swallow of champagne to moisten her throat, and as Liam rounded the corner of the dining-area, she raised her glass to him in a mock toast.

'Well, well! Look who we have here!' she said in deliberate parody of the words he had used to greet her in Mr Jepherson's office.

His face was pale and strained with fatigue, but his smile was as devastating as ever. 'Gina . . .' he murmued, his eyes gloating over her.

'You remember me,' she tossed at him sarcastically.

'I love you,' he said with a deep throb that was almost her undoing.

She slammed her glass down on the wide granite coffee-table which separated the two leather sofas, and glared up at him in furious resentment. 'You don't know the meaning of the word love, Liam Shannon. And if you think the wounded hero bit is going to melt me, you can think again.'

His smile did not falter. 'You look ravishing in red.'

She jumped up in a burst of seething frustration. 'You're nothing but a self-centred glory-seeker!' she yelled at him.

'You are incredibly beautiful when you're angry. Your eyes sparkle like green fire . . .' He was coming towards her.

'Don't you come near me!' she cried, dodging to the far side of the table. 'I've got a lot to say to you, and you're going to listen, if you know what's good for you.'

He shrugged off his coat and dropped it on the sofa. His lips pursed into a teasing quirk. 'Oh, I think I know what would be good for me. I've been thinking of nothing else for days.'

Gina's blood over-heated, whether from boiling rage or the look in his eyes, she wasn't sure, but she stubbornly kept moving out of his range as he followed her around the table.

'I will not be forced this time, Liam Shannon!' she snarled at him. 'And I won't wait around for your convenience while you gallivant around the world taking stupid risks with your life. This has got to stop right now! I won't put up with it.'

'Say you love me,' he purred at her, unbuttoning his shirt in a disturbingly provocative manner.

'I will not! You enjoyed it, didn't you?' she accused bitterly. 'You could have called off this one last job if you'd wanted to. You didn't have to go and risk your neck.'

He grinned. 'My darling, I was always lucky when you hated me. But this time my luck ran out. That's convincing proof that you love me. I wanted to find out, and I did. Conclusively.'

Gina bared her teeth. 'You've never grown up, Liam Shannon. You're just as wild as you ever were. Wild and irresponsible! And you lied to me!'

'Never!'

'You said your business was respectable.'

'What could be more respectable than giving culture to the world?'

'In a pig's eye! You can twist anything, Liam Shannon! I'll never be able to trust your word again!'

Liam lifted his hands in innocent appeal. 'What trust have I broken? I said nothing could stop me from coming back to you, and here I am, my heart.'

'Your heart, indeed!' Gina scoffed, totally unappeased. 'I know where your heart is! You can't bear not to have the excitement of danger and...'

'I've never been more excited than I am now. I know it's dangerous, but so long as you make love to me, Gina, I swear I'll never think of anything else.'

'We can't spend the rest of our lives in bed!'

'It's worth a try.'

She stamped her foot in frustration. 'Liam, you're not listening to me.'

'Yes, I am, darling. Your voice is like music to my ears.'

'Why did you do it?' she screeched at him.

His smile held a tilt of self-mockery. 'It seemed like a good idea at the time.'

He pulled off his shirt, and Gina's eyes fastened on the gauze and plaster dressing just below his left shoulder. A frisson of horror ran down her spine. If the wound had been a few inches lower... She gulped and flew back on attack. 'You could have been killed! And for what?'

He cocked an appealing eyebrow at her. 'Well, I thought twenty million dollars was a good round figure.'

'Twenty...'

He almost caught her, but she recovered in time to fend him away. For some reason she was breathing hard as she evaded him.

'That's no excuse!' she panted. 'We don't need that kind of money.'

'Of course we don't,' he soothed. 'But you did tell me there was no public fund to help kids like Debbie, remember? So when Vincente approached me with the deal the day after...' he grimaced '...after I'd messed everything up with you, I thought it was something useful I could do.'

The day after... When he believed... when her ill-tamed revelation about Debbie had reinforced his belief that she had sold herself to get the money...

'I thought there were probably other parents like you who couldn't afford to give their children the medical treatment to set them right,' Liam kept on explaining. He offered her an appealing smile. 'How does *The Gina Shannon Salvation Fund* sound to you? The doctors at Camperdown Hospital could administer it.'

When he got no immediate response from her, he shrugged. 'Anyway, I thought it was a great idea.'

Gina tried to steady her whirling thoughts. 'You did it... for all the children that could be helped?'

He nodded. 'It means that never again will anyone go blind for lack of money.'

She was stunned into immobility, and Liam stepped slowly forward and slid his hands around her waist. Gina looked up at him, helplessly drowning in the soft blue eyes that had suddenly deepened to dark fathomless pools of love.

'I wanted to do something that might make me worthy of you, Gina,' he said softly.

'Worthy?' She shook her head in total confusion. 'I don't understand, Liam.'

'You stood by Jim when I deserted him. You made enormous sacrifices for Debbie's sake. And I... I've lived for no one but myself. Even with you... you were right when you said I didn't know the meaning of love, Gina. I've felt so deeply shamed by the selfish, mean-hearted way I've treated you, my darling. I thought if I could give, as you have given... I know it's only money...'

'But you risked your life for it,' she whispered, all her anger totally shattered.

'That wasn't in the plan, Gina, I promise you,' he answered very solemnly.

She was both appalled and humbled by his gesture, a gesture so extreme and so characteristic of this extraordinary man she loved that apprehension squeezed her heart. 'Liam, please... you won't get involved in something like this again?'

'My last job, Gina. I swear it.'

And she believed him. She wrapped her arms around him and softly pressed her lips to his injured shoulder, her heart pounding a prayer of relief and gratitude that he had lived to come back to her. 'I love you, Liam,' she breathed on a long, quivering sigh. 'I couldn't bear it if you died on me.'

A slight shudder ran through him, and he pressed her closer, his hands running possessively over the soft sway of her back. 'You are home to me, Gina. I'll never leave you again.'

'Home...' Gina echoed contentedly.

His lips moved warmly over her hair. 'I said once that I only wanted your beautiful body, but that's not true, Gina. It never was true. It's the person you are. You have an inner strength, a quality of endurance that defies everything else. You decide what is right and you carry it through, no matter how much it hurts you.'

He sighed and smiled down at her. 'You have a steadfastness... we complement one another, you know. We need each other's strengths to eliminate the weaknesses. We belong together, and together, my darling, we are invincible.'

His smile tilted with irony. 'I guess I knew in my heart of hearts that you would stay with Jim. It *was* too late... and I didn't want to hurt Jim, either. And as much as I hated you for it, Gina, I admired the rigid loyalty that turned me away. The hell of it was... I knew why Jim loved you. For the same reason I did. We both instinctively recognised that you were the woman who could give our rootless, floating lives the fulfilment we craved...'

'Liam...' His words had turned a knife of guilt. 'I think I failed Jim. I...'

He shook his head. 'He was wrong for you, Gina. I know, without your telling me, that you did your best for him. And no one could have done better. He was my best friend, and I loved him... but Jim could never work out any direction for himself. He had to be carried along. He left you with all the burdens of responsibility, didn't he?'

'Yes,' she whispered, loving him all the more for his understanding.

'I'm not irresponsible, Gina. Not always wise. But I've never failed to carry my load. And others', whenever there was need for it.'

'I know.' She reached up and impulsively stroked his cheek. 'I know, Liam.'

She remembered Bruno telling her that Liam had been helping a friend when he was shot, and Gina knew he would never let anyone down if he could help in any way whatsoever. Like the money for Debbie. The twenty million dollars for handicapped children.

Liam would make it big, Jim had said, and now she knew the full truth. Maybe she had always known it in the hidden recesses of her mind. Liam could never do anything else but make it big. He had a heart as large as Esme's, and she loved him for all that he was.

The things he'd done—getting refugees out— Gina wondered how many had never paid a cent for Liam's services. And the gun-running...she was sure it would have been to people who had the right to survive and fight for justice. For all Liam said he wasn't proud of some of his past activites, Gina was certain there were many, many people who were grateful to him.

She smiled with all the love that was brimming from her heart. 'I think I should take you to bed and keep you there where I know you're safe.'

His face relaxed into a wide grin. 'I refuse to be safe in bed. There I can only be wild and...oh, no!' He looked at her in anguish. 'What did the doctor say when he saw you?'

She laughed, bubbling with joy and happiness. 'Your child is behaving itself. Now all I've go to do is make you behave.'

'You'll find me very co-operative,' he promised wickedly. 'More ready than I've ever been in my life, enthusiastically willing, and so able I can hardly wait.'

'How about your shoulder?' she asked anxiously as he led her towards the bed.

'If you promise not to bite it, I'll manage very nicely.'

'I'll try to remember.'

'I'll forgive you, anyway.'

They turned to each other, the lightness of their words belied by the hungry need in their eyes. In mutual accord, they moved into an embrace of intense feeling, clinging to each other in a long, silent ecstasy of belonging...this is my man, this is my woman...and nothing could ever sunder the love that pulsed between them with every vibrant beat of their hearts.

Liam had come home, and Gina silently vowed that she would keep the fires burning into eternity for this man. No matter what he did, or however extreme or wild he was, he was the man she wanted, needed, loved; and no one else ever—in any way—could possibly fill his place in her heart.

CHAPTER ELEVEN

LIAM insisted on taking her and Debbie shopping the next morning, and he steered them straight to one of the most exclusive bridal salons in the city. Debbie was in seventh heaven trying on the most exquisite flower-girl outfits, and Gina was absolutely overwhelmed with magnificent wedding gowns.

'But, Liam,' she protested in an embarrassed whisper, 'aren't we getting married in a register office?'

'Certainly not. Three o'clock this afternoon at the Wayside Chapel. I've ordered all the flowers. Got my morning-suit ready to wear. And you, my darling, will be the bride I've been waiting for all my life.'

And the joyful anticipation in his eyes stilled any further protest. What matter that she had been married before... or even that she was three months pregnant? This was the wedding of their lives, and Liam was right. It deserved every possible celebration.

The marriage service was a very simple one, attended only by Esme and Bruno, but the chapel was awash with flowers, the flower-girl sparkled with happy excitement, the bride glowed with a very special beauty, and the groom was the epitome of love triumphant.

Gina and Liam exchanged their marriage vows with a fervour that brought tears to Esme's eyes. She had to hug Bruno's arm to express some of her emotion. He patted her hand, inwardly relieved that Gina had forgiven him—it was obvious that she didn't understand or appreciate great art—and even more relieved that his Esme had not thought him stupid at all. His pleasure in Gina and Liam's marriage was compounded by Esme's promise that she would now come to Italy with him.

As soon as the ceremony was completed, Debbie turned to Liam with her own private sense of triumph. 'And now you're my daddy, arent you?' she said exultantly.

He scooped her up with his good arm. 'I sure am, sweetheart. To have and to hold from this day forth.'

Debbie threw her arms around his neck and kissed him loudly on the cheek. 'I do so love you, Liam.'

His eyes met Gina's over their daughter's head, and they smiled, and in that moment all the pain and torment of the past was wiped out for ever. They would share a future where they would always be together, and their children would always be certain of their love.

It seemed, for the first time in her life, that Gina had no worries. She and Liam and Debbie flew to Athens, then boarded the yacht for a long, blissful cruise around the Greek Islands. For two months they did nothing but enjoy themselves in any way that took their fancy.

Gina's pregnancy gave her no trouble at all, but, as the baby grew and her condition became very obvious, Gina could not stifle one little worry that nagged at her mind. Finally she felt she had to clear the matter away, but it took all her courage to bring it out into the open.

'Liam...' She searched his eyes anxiously as she forced the necessary words out. 'You don't have any doubts that the baby is yours?'

His incredulous look was reassuring. 'Gina, you can't think... Good God! I have no doubts at all. I'm absolutely certain that I'm the father.'

She sighed her relief.

His mouth curled into an ironic little smile and he shook his head at her. 'You really should read the newspapers.'

'What have I missed this time?' she asked.

'You can prove maternity and paternity these days. DNA tests. Same principle as fingerprints. If it will set your mind at rest, Gina, I can easily have my paternity certified, but believe me, there's no doubt in my mind. Never has been. Never will be.'

And he took her in his arms and kissed her with an eloquent conviction that made nonsense of such a needless worry.

'We're so lucky to have each other, aren't we?' Gina breathed ecstatically. 'When I think if you hadn't pressed the wrong button in the elevator...'

'Well...umm...' Liam cleared his throat and looked embarrassed. 'You've got to understand,

Gina, it was a severe case of pride at the time. You weren't giving me any encouragement...'

'Are you telling me you lied, Liam Shannon?' Gina pounced, her eyes teasing him unmercifully.

'Only that once,' he insisted. 'I'd known for some time that you worked for Jepherson's, and I was torn with the temptation to see you, to find out if you were happy in your marriage to Jim. My resolve to keep clear of you finally cracked. I promised myself I would only look. But when I saw you, I couldn't tear myself away. And I still can't,' he grinned, and kissed her again.

It was quite some time later that Gina thought to ask how he had known that she worked at Jepherson's.

'My accountant,' Liam answered, his eyes teasing her as he explained further. 'He actually does work in that building and he was smitten with you. If it hadn't been for Jim's ring on your finger, he would have been chasing you.'

Gina shook her head in bemusement. 'So it wasn't fate, after all.'

'No. It was only a matter of time, my love,' Liam said with moving simplicity.

'I'm glad of that,' Gina sighed contentedly. 'I never liked the thought that we might have missed each other.'

'I would have made some enquiry about you and Jim sooner or later, Gina. When I thought I could cope with it. And once I knew you were no longer tied to Jim...'

'You would have swept in and forced me to see the light.'

He slanted an eyebrow at her. 'Are you telling me now that you didn't mind the forcing, Gina Shannon?'

'Well . . . umm . . . sometimes the end does justify the means,' she declared, thinking how very right 'Gina Shannon' sounded when Liam said it.

Esme and Bruno invited them to stay a while at Bruno's villa on Capri. It was a beautiful place, cut into a rocky and steep hill, overlooking flowering glades, terraced vineyards, and all the flat-roofed, chalk-white houses that spilled down to the translucent azure water of the Bay of Naples.

'It is the most romantic place in the world,' Esme enthused. 'I am so inspired . . .'

And Bruno proudly showed off all her new paintings, which were more stunning than ever.

The villa was spacious, cool, casually elegant with its marble floors, charming furniture, niches that displayed sculptures and graceful vases, windows framed in bougainvillaea or oleanders, terraces and verdant outdoor gardens. Gina and Liam were given a private suite, and Debbie was delighted to have Esme's company again.

Gina was particularly keen to explore the island, because her grandmother had been born there and had been very fond of telling her granddaughter all about it. With Gina's knowledge of Italian, she had no trouble getting on with the local people, and Debbie picked up a smattering of the language with surprising ease.

They spent two wonderful weeks there, and just as Gina was beginning to feel a bit homesick for Australia, and wishing that she and Liam could have a settled home of their own, her new husband dropped a large envelope in her lap. 'Something that I thought might be good. Tell me what you think,' he invited, his eyes twinkling in mischievous anticipation.

The envelope contained photographs of a lovely sprawling country home, with barns and stables and beautiful green pastures where horses and foals were grazing.

'I've had an agent looking for a stud farm,' Liam explained. 'Always fancied breeding horses. Good country life for the kids,' he suggested artfully.

'I love it!' Gina cried. 'Oh, Liam! It's a marvellous idea!'

'Then you'll be happy if we buy it and settle down there?'

She threw her arms around him in an ecstatic hug. 'I'd love you anywhere.'

'But home is best,' he grinned, then kissed her with a fervour that told her without any more words that he instinctively knew her needs and would always satisfy them.

They stayed at Capri to see Esme and Bruno married, and Liam surprised and delighted Gina once again by purchasing a house not far from Bruno's villa. 'It's just as well to have a home here, too,' Liam declared. 'So you can come and see Esme whenever you want.'

There were no words to express her perfect contentment. She was so rich now, not only materially, but in far more important ways. To have Liam, to watch Debbie's eyes lighting up at everything in sight, to see Esme so happy with Bruno, to be expecting Liam's child...she was indeed rich beyond her wildest dreams.

When they flew home to Australia, they were immediately captivated by the property the agent had found for Liam. It was precisely what they wanted: ideal for the horses that interested Liam, in easy driving distance of Sydney, and close to a good local school for Debbie.

Gina was absolutely thrilled with the house. She took months over the furnishings—getting just the right country touch—and it still wasn't entirely finished when the baby interrupted everything.

Debbie happily stayed with a friendly neighbour while Liam took Gina to the hospital and sat with her in the delivery-room. He didn't leave her for a second, holding her hand tightly, giving supportive encouragement as she suffered through the labour. When the baby was finally born, he heaved a huge sigh of relief.

'That's the greatest ordeal I've ever been through. You're not to have any more babies, Gina.'

'We'll see,' she smiled—and that from a man who had risked death a thousand times!

'It's a boy,' the doctor announced.

Liam squeezed Gina's hand. 'A boy,' he echoed with loving pride.

Gina sighed in resignation. 'It would have to be a boy.'

Liam looked anxiously at her. 'You wanted a girl?'

She smiled away the question. 'Maybe he'll find enough excitement with horses. Without going gliding or...'

Liam laughed and dropped a kiss on her forehead. 'He's your son, my love. There's hope for him.'

But when the doctor laid her new-born son in her arms, Gina looked down at the slight dimple in his chin and shook her head in bemusement. 'I don't know, Liam. He looks awfully like you.'

'Debbie will whip him into shape in no time,' Liam declared. 'The family will rule.'

Family...it was what Liam had never had...what she could give him. And would give him, even if it was an ordeal for him to sit through each birth. He would just have to get used to it. After all, it was only a day, and then they were rewarded with a beautiful baby. Gina's heart swelled with happiness as she looked from her son to her husband.

'I do so love you, Liam,' she sighed.

'Gina...'

He didn't have to say more. The way he said her name...the whole wealth of life and love was in it. And when his lips brushed softly over hers, it was the mingling of two people who had truly shared everything...and become one.

Coming Next Month

Available in July wherever paperback books are sold, or through Harlequin Reader Service:

In the U.S.
901 Fuhrmann Blvd.
P.O. Box 1397
Buffalo, N.Y. 14240-1397

In Canada
P.O. Box 603
Fort Erie, Ontario
L2A 5X3

Janet DAILEY

THE MASTER FIDDLER

Jacqui didn't want to go back to college, and she didn't want to go home. Tombstone, Arizona, wasn't in her plans, either, until she found herself stuck there en route to L.A. after ramming her car into rancher Choya Barnett's Jeep. Things got worse when she lost her wallet and couldn't pay for the repairs. The mechanic wasn't interested when she practically propositioned him to get her car back—but Choya was. He took care of her bills and then waited for the debt to be paid with the only thing Jacqui had to offer—her virtue.

Watch for this bestselling Janet Dailey favorite, coming in June from Harlequin.

Also watch for *Something Extra* in August and *Sweet Promise* in October.

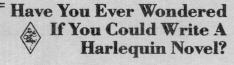

Have You Ever Wondered
If You Could Write A
Harlequin Novel?

Here's great news—Harlequin
is offering a series of cassette
tapes to help you do just that.
Written by Harlequin editors,
these tapes give practical
advice on how to make your
characters—and your story—
come alive. There's a tape for
each contemporary romance
series Harlequin publishes.

Mail order only

All sales final

ANNOUNCING . . .

The Lost Moon Flower
by Bethany Campbell

Look for it this August
wherever Harlequins are sold

HR 3000-1